PHANTOMS

ALSO BY CHRISTIAN KIEFER

One Day Soon Time Will
Have No Place Left to Hide

The Animals

The Infinite Tides

PHANTOMS

a novel

CHRISTIAN KIEFER

LIVERIGHT PUBLISHING CORPORATION
A Division of W. W. Norton & Company
Independent Publishers Since 1923
NEW YORK   LONDON

Excerpt from *The Sorrow of War: A Novel of North Vietnam* by Bảo Ninh, copyright © 1995 by Bảo Ninh. Used by permission of Pantheon Books, an imprint of the Knopf Doubleday Publishing Group, a division of Penguin Random House LLC. All rights reserved.

California State Mining Bureau. Placer County California. [S.l.: s.n, 1902] Map. https://www.loc.gov/item/2007633931/.

For information about permission to reproduce selections from this book, write to Permissions, Liveright Publishing Corporation, a division of W. W. Norton & Company, Inc., 500 Fifth Avenue, New York, NY 10110

For information about special discounts for bulk purchases, please contact W. W. Norton Special Sales at specialsales@wwnorton.com or 800-233-4830

Manufacturing by Worzalla Publishing Company
Book design by Barbara Bachman
Production manager: Beth Steidle

Library of Congress Cataloging-in-Publication Data

Names: Kiefer, Christian, 1971– author.
Title: Phantoms : a novel / Christian Kiefer.
Description: First edition. | New York : Liveright Publishing Corporation, [2019]
Identifiers: LCCN 2018044996 | ISBN 9780871404817 (hardcover)
Classification: LCC PS3611.I443 P48 2019 | DDC 813/.6—dc23
LC record available at https://lccn.loc.gov/2018044996

Liveright Publishing Corporation, 500 Fifth Avenue, New York, N.Y. 10110
www.wwnorton.com

W. W. Norton & Company Ltd., 15 Carlisle Street, London W1D 3BS

1 2 3 4 5 6 7 8 9 0

*Respectfully dedicated to the following individuals
and families, removed from their homes in Newcastle,
California and interred at Tule Lake, May 1942:*

Asazawa	Kurosawa	Ooka
Daijogo	Kushida	Osaki
Endo	Masuda	Saeki
Enkoji	Matsuda	Sukai
Hada	Matsumoto	Sakakihara
Hamaoka	Mitani	Sakamoto
Harada	Moriguchi	Sakatani
Hashiguchi	Muraoka	Shinkawa
Hikida	Nagafuji	Sunada
Hirabayashi	Nakadoi	Tahara
Hiraiwa	Nakagawa	Takata
Hiranaka	Nakamura	Tanaka
Hironaka	Nakao	Tanihana
Hirota	Nakashima	Tanno
Hirozawa	Nakata	Tokutomi
Horiuchi	Nakatomi	Tomita
Ichikawa	Nakayama	Uyeno
Imamoto	Namba	Watanabe
Itano	Nimura	Yamane
Kanda	Nishikawa	Yasuda
Kawahata	Noda	Yokota
Kawayoshi	Nodohara	Yonemura
Kojima	Nomura	Yoshida
Kono	Okusako	Yoshikawa
Kurimoto	Omoto	Yoshimoto

The sorrow of war inside a soldier's heart was in a strange way similar to the sorrow of love. It was a kind of nostalgia, like the immense sadness of a world at dusk. It was a sadness, a missing, a pain which could send one soaring back into the past.

—BẢO NINH

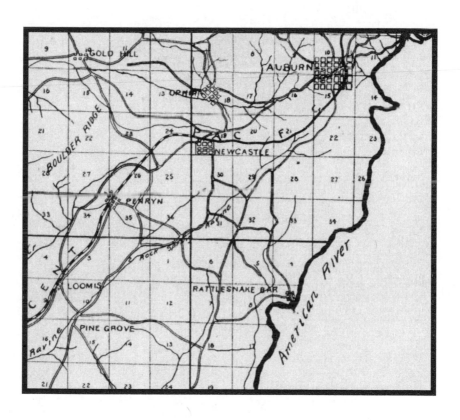

PHANTOMS

1

RAY TAKAHASHI RETURNED IN AUGUST. BY THEN WE HAD put the whole thing behind us, or tried to, whatever concern or even guilt we might have felt replaced by that mixture of jubilation and despair brought on by the war's end, for our boys were coming home and the war had changed them. Some held only absence where an arm or leg had once been; some were broken by experiences we could not see and never would. And of course others did not return at all, families receiving a Western Union telegram signed by a general of whom none of us had heard. Later would come the casket and the folded flag. But these were eddies of respectful quietude in a flow of celebration: parades and confetti and flags and bunting and a sense that we had done something honorable, that our boys had tested their mettle in Europe and the Pacific and had been rewarded with victory. We were proud of them. We were proud of ourselves.

Frank Marston was the first to see Ray Takahashi that day—a soldier, small of stature, stepping down from the penultimate train car and into the bright eddying dust of the town square—and it was Marston who, much later, would comment on just how ordinary that train had been: the same as the train that had stopped alongside the fruit sheds the day before and the same as the train that would arrive the day after, its cars empty to receive the stacks of crated peaches and plums and pears that rose in compact towers from the dark interior of that long, bustling room. Indeed, as the locomotive's roar descended into its low idling rattle, the workmen of that day were already slipping into their gloves in the air of diesel fumes and oil and the ever-present cloying scent of the fruit itself.

Ray Takahashi's beauty had always been tragic and heroic but upon his return that tragedy and heroism felt real in ways that before had been only imaginary. His hair, once swept back in a shining black wave, was shorn close now, and his thin, lithe body, always tight and muscled, had become, somehow, even harder than it might have after a season in the orchards, his skin as tan as ours, but his gaze somehow more distant, as if he was, even as he looked in our direction, gazing past us into some landscape we could not see and never would, not the boy who had gone away but a man now, a soldier who stared through the shimmering air into the darkness of the sheds from which, even as he struggled to pull shapes from the sunlit glare, came the floor lady's high peal—"All right, you lazybones. Let's get at 'em"—and he knew, he must have known, without having to see them, that the workers had begun the process of loading the cars. August meant that peaches were coming to an end, replaced by the season's first pears and plums, a fact he also would have known, a knowledge and understanding that ran deep in his bones and blood the same as it did for all of us, the smell of it—a mix of fresh sugar and sweet decay—like the smell of his own toil across all the summers of his youth. For a long trembling moment he simply stood there in the shadows, watching the shapes of the loaders move back and forth from the crates to the cars and back again. "Christ I wanna get home," one of the soldiers mumbled from inside the car. "Christ I just wanna get home."

The dust around his feet. The scent upon the air. Frank Marston's shape must have appeared a black specter stepping through from one world to the next. "Welcome home, soldier," he said.

"Thanks, Mr. Marston."

And now Frank Marston pulled up short. For a time he could only stare goggle-eyed at the uniform before him, the recognition dawning on him slowly so that his dull eyes, shadowed now by the train car itself, began to spark even as the great engine coughed and clanked in its rumbling idle.

"Well hell, it's Tak's boy," he said at last. He paused and then added the name as it came to his mind: "Ray. Didn't recognize you in that uniform," already stepping forward, his mouth curling in an idiot's broad grin, hand outstretched.

Ray took it in his own and when they were done Marston stepped back and looked him up and down, nodding. "I think I read that they let some of you sign up," he said.

"Some of who?" This voice from the train car, one of the soldiers staring from the window at the two men below, eyes half closed as if only partially bothering to wake.

Marston looked up and then back to Ray and then up to the window again. "Ah you know," he said. "I just meant—well hell, this boy's pop and I go way back. Don't we?"

"Sure, sure, Mr. Marston," Ray said. He waved a hand at the window. The soldier there shrugged but did not return to his seat, instead continuing to peer down at the two men, his jaw working a stale lump of chewing gum all the while.

Frank Marston had begun nodding and now it seemed as if he could not stop. "Well hell, Ray," he said at last, glancing down at him and then at the window and then at Ray once more. "I'm glad to see you back safe and sound."

"It's good to be home," he said simply.

They stood together, the two men, for a beat and then another, Ray staring at Marston and the man at first returning his unwavering gaze and then dropping his eyes to the dust itself.

"I'll be off then," Ray said.

"You're not—" Marston began, cutting off his own sentence and then starting again, "I mean—" and then cutting off that second attempt just as the floor lady called his name from some-where inside the sheds: "Frank? Where's Frank?" and Marston turned toward that sound, just for the briefest moment. When he turned back to Ray Takahashi it was to find the soldier walk-ing without haste down the dusty street, his head slowly rotating from one side to the other as if taking in the scene before him: the dirt-and-gravel clearing that acted as the town's main square, its surface flanked by the long low metal-roofed fruit sheds and, opposite them, the small collection of structures that made up the town, clean box-like homes and occasional older Victori-ans. Among them grew oaks and the gray twisted shapes of dig-ger pines and, here and there, an otherwise out-of-place palm, planted in some lost time to denote a status long forgotten.

As if the whole topography from the air: each ripple of the land distinct and clear and named and owned and perfect, a

geography that knit us together in ways we did not even understand until the war was over. In the draw, the little ramshackle
Japantown huddled in the shade of the cottonwoods, above
which rose the slopes of the Tokutomis' orchard upon the flanks
of Chantry Hill. To the southwest the ridges ran in descending
waves toward the Buddhist church at Penryn and the Methodist
church at Loomis, towns no larger than Newcastle itself and yet
focal because of the Sunday gatherings where they would dress
in their finery and which they looked forward to, not because
of the service but because it allowed them each a chance to see
their Sunday friends, especially the children, sharing the curious experience of growing up in America and Japan simultaneously, this push and pull the tide of their lives. It was all still
here, at least physically, seemingly unchanged even after everything that had happened.

On the turning gravel road Ray would have appeared to
be, at least at a distance, just another soldier trudging home,
first down to the irrigation canal and then west to cut into the
edge of the rising ridgeline, oaks casting their shadows east-
ward across the tops of the yellow grasses, the occasional truck
passing along the dirt, some slowing to look him over, this olive-
clad soldier with his duffel. Perhaps one stopped to offer him
a ride simply because he was a soldier and the soldiers were
coming home, but he would not have taken such a ride, would
have nodded politely and demurred, would have told them that
he wanted to feel the road under his feet, to test the quality of
the air, to feel that he was no longer in some dream or fantasy
but had once more returned to the land of his birth. How many
times had he walked along the dirt road up the side of the ridge,
and how many times had he come down that same road with

Jimmy and sometimes with Helen too, in Mr. Wilson's borrowed Ford, all the way down the hill to the confluence of the
river, feeling in all those years that he was not different at all,
that they were simply young people living their lives? But of
course it was exactly this that had been proven a lie. First there
had been Tule Lake and then, after he had enlisted, Mississippi
for training and then Anzio and the grim terror of the war. He
had volunteered as a measure against everything that had come
upon his father and his mother and his two sisters, as if in choosing he could somehow wash away every choice he had been
unable to make. Maybe the gravel road up the ridge should have
been filled with mines and machine gun nests. If it had been, it
would not have been any more surprising than its current state
and condition of being exactly identical to his memory.

So maybe when he came into the dooryard and saw, at long
last, the faces of strangers, white faces, in the dusty windows of
the only home he had ever known, maybe then it finally began
to feel real. There stood the home in which he had grown up, a
small rectangular box, white-painted—Ray and his father and
Jimmy Wilson had made a short day of that work while Ray's
sisters and mother supplied them with lemonade—with a grass
yard and the shade tree upon which the tire swing still hung.
Behind it he could see the first row of the five acres of plum
trees his father had planted when Ray had been a boy of six
or seven, their shapes now gnarled and battered with age. His
father had intended that they be removed and replanted, work
they had begun together in 1941, the year before Tule Lake.
They had pulled the trees at the back edge of the property and
replanted them with saplings. That the rest of the work had
been neglected, that the faces of strangers had appeared and

now reappeared in the windows, these facts only increased the sense of outrage building in his chest moment by moment until he thought the accumulation would burst clean of him altogether. But like the soldiers in the train car his eyes told nothing, not the stare of some caricatured Asian, stoic and enduring in the face of loss and hardship—gaman, his father might have called it—but the eyes of a soldier, a soldier who had survived Anzio and the horror of the Vosges Mountains and Bruyères and the Gothic Line and all the rest, survived when so many others had bled out into European soil that held no meaning for any of them whatsoever.

He already knew what he would find there, that they were simply tenants upon land owned not by his father or by himself but by Homer Wilson, a plot that the Wilsons had rented them as part of a shared agreement, some percentage of the harvest's yield. So they did not own it but it was still the Takahashi family home. None of us would have denied it had we been asked and yet Tak also would have accepted—did accept—the right of Homer Wilson to rent it to someone else, a right as unalienable, as *American*, as our right to food, to water, to air. Tak would have accepted it but Ray would not, did not.

"Who are you?"

A young woman had come around from the back of the little house and stood now partially shielded by the dusty and rust-spotted vehicle parked in the dooryard. She was a few years older than Ray, her hair the color of old straw and her face so thin as to appear drawn.

"Ray," he said. "I'm Ray."

"You just . . . ," she began. Then she said, quickly, "My husband's just in back."

He looked at her, kept looking at her even when she turned her eyes away. "How long you been living here?" he said.

"What do you want?"

"I'm just looking," he said. And he was, his eyes following the shape of her as one might follow the shape of a candle flame in a dark room, his gaze not unlike that which had met Frank Marston in the shadow of the fruit shed, unwavering and focused, his attention so complete as to be utterly unnerving, threatening only in the fact that he would not look away.

"He's just in back," she said again before breaking with a quick, jerking pace, away from him. Then the bang of the back door, the screen. How strange that some woman he did not know had made that sound, not his mother nor his sisters nor even his father. Not Jimmy or Helen either. Through the window the two young faces he had seen when he first approached the house peered out at him with frank curiosity until the curtains were pulled roughly into position.

That this would be his homecoming could not have been a surprise. Although we did not know the specifics we knew at least that he would have corresponded with his father during the war years and that, if nothing else, Tak would have told his son that the family would not be found in the orchard beside the Wilsons' ranch but instead in Oakland, where they were unceremoniously crammed into the apartment of a distant relative Ray had never met. Perhaps this had been his imagined destination when he had been in Europe, the remains of his unit waiting in Nice under the full hot Mediterranean sun. But something changed in the days of waiting in France and during the long sultry summer that followed after they had at last been loaded aboard the Liberty ship that took him first to Fort

Dix and then, via lucky happenstance, to an empty seat aboard a military transport crossing the continent from east to west in leaps and fits. After changing planes and cargo trucks and planes again, he found himself in California once more, first at Camp Pendleton and then, again via lucky happenstance, on a ship bound for Fort Mason in San Francisco, arriving there in August to the news that a bomb of epic destructive power had been loosed upon the Japanese city of Hiroshima.

Had we considered him at all, we might have expected him to go immediately to his family, but after all those days of travel from France to New York to San Diego to San Francisco, all those days of thinking, of pondering what his father had written him, he did exactly the opposite of what any of us would have expected, exactly the opposite even of what his father might have expected, not traveling immediately to Oakland to meet his family or even to Newcastle but instead remaining in San Francisco for a full day and then another, not at the army base either but in a flophouse near the docks where prostitutes and foreign sailors were known to comingle openly and without fear of arrest, all the while close enough to his father and mother and sisters that a leisurely walk of three or four hours might well have brought him to their new address. Even if they had no phone he might have reached a neighbor or a corner store and relayed a message, but no call came and so the parents did not even know that their son had returned home, or at least had returned to the country that had been his home, even though now there was no actual physical home to speak of, a fact made clear by the note that had arrived in his father's hand and in clear, unambiguous English: *We are no longer welcome at our old home in Newcastle. We have no friends there now. Find us at Cousin*

Ida's. The address followed but it may as well have been written in German or Italian or even in Japanese, a language he could hardly speak and could not read at all. We are no longer welcome. We have no friends there now. Impossible.

And yet there was, even in his route, a sense of caution. Perhaps seeing, with his own eyes, that straw-haired woman and her children had made his father's letter real to him, for before the removal, before the summer of 1942, Ray would have simply walked down the rows along a path worn not only by him and his father and mother and his two sisters but by Mr. Wilson and Helen and Jimmy too: down a single row of peach trees in a straight line, veering off to the left toward the Wilsons' back door only after it reached the end of the row. But the spring of 1942 had come and gone and 1943 and 1944 too and now it was August and the war was over—the war in Europe and now, with the second atomic bomb, the war against Japan—and so although he could still see it in the grass between the trees, in actuality the path might as well have not been there at all.

So he did not take that route but turned on his heel and walked back through the green leaves and the heat to the road. He could see the whole of the country to the north from that point, the hills that flowed up the side of Auburn Ravine, their shapes covered, acre after acre, with the ordered rows of orchard trees and through which he could make out the snug pale homes of the farmers themselves. He knew they would still be picking the late peaches and plums and the first of the pears but he could make out none of that activity from the road. The whole spread of the landscape to the north seemed something he might have dreamed—and there it was again, the idea that he was somehow asleep and dreaming all this even though it was right here, present and alive. The breeze blew up the ridge from the south, up Red Ravine and across the orchards that lined the county road to the sheds at Penryn and Loomis and the quarries of Rocklin and on to the great railyards at Roseville, a place he had seen only once, that very day when his train from San Francisco had slowed and paused there as the tracks were switched. Even now the train rattled on up the mountain: Dutch Flat and Donner Summit and the great mythic blue of Tahoe before plunging into the high desert beyond. He had been at Bruyères near a year ago and now he was here, home again, although of course already it seemed less home than it ever had been. How alone he must have looked there.

The Wilsons' drive appeared just as everything else did, so exactly matching his memory that it seemed utterly false, the dark leaves that lined the road perfectly still. The back of his shirt had soaked through an hour ago and remained wet and hot against his flesh, the duffel burden enough that he slung it to the side of the road against the low trunk of a peach tree long since harvested clean.

The first of the pickers appeared when the bare peach trees changed to pears heavy with late summer fruit, and he glanced down the rows to see ladders disappearing into the upper branches. He did not stand to watch, instead quickening his pace so that he was nearly at march step. He could sense them watching him now and although he could not identify any clear reason for his own sense of disquiet, he did not return their gaze, only continuing to walk as their chatter diminished, their eyes upon him, this uniformed soldier.

And then his name, called from behind in a voice cheerful and bright, and he turned to that sound even though it felt as if doing so might augur into place a future he did not want to accept.

The boy who stood before him was a teen, his head topped with a tousle of yellow hair. "It's me," he said when Ray did not respond, his mouth curling into a full broad smile. "Bish Kenner. Bishop, I mean. You forget me, Ray?"

"Bish," Ray said quietly. "Sure. You're just a lot bigger than the last I saw you."

"Well, I am," he said. "'Most fifteen."

"Well, good," Ray said.

"You were in the fightin'?"

"Some."

"In Japan?" The words came quickly but then the boy seemed embarrassed, for he looked away quickly, his sharp shoulders seeming to jump up and down for a moment, a kind of oblique apology.

"No, not in Japan," Ray said. "Italy and France, mostly."

"No kidding," the boy said, his embarrassment gone now. "My brother went to the Pacific. Okinawa."

"That so? How's he?"

"Got back about a month ago. Japs took his leg." He paused. "Ah jeez. I didn't mean it like that."

"You don't gotta apologize," Ray said. "Goddamn Japs took Chet's leg. To hell with them, I say."

The boy laughed at this response, relieved. In the group behind the boy Ray could see a few others smiling at his words. "Yeah, to hell with the goddamn Japs," Bish said with apparent glee. "To hell with them."

"Listen," Ray said, "you tell Chet I said hello, would you?"

"I will," the boy said, still smiling.

"What the hell's going on?"

"Ray's back," Bish called into the trees.

"I don't care if Jesus himself has returned," the voice came, closer now, heading down through the hot rows of pear trees, "you all'd better get moving."

The pickers—young men and women, most of whom Ray recognized in one way or another from the high school—had already begun scrambling back into the trees or to the truck to gently spill their loads into the pears already waiting there. Bish was the last to flee, finally waving silently and disappearing just as the foreman—for of course it was the foreman—appeared from between the rows.

Ray did not recognize him at first, a thin, gruff-voiced man of perhaps thirty-five, clean-shaven and wearing a tan cap upon what appeared to be a stubbled scalp. But then the features came into focus and he said the man's name: "Bob Campo."

"That's right," Campo said. "What's your business?"

"Heading up to the house," Ray told him.

"I'm gonna give you one more chance to tell me what you're doing here and then . . ."

"And then what, Bob?"

Ray did not wait for a response but turned and continued on his way.

So quiet were the orchard rows. So fired with summer heat. It came up from the earth. It flooded through them all.

"I won't be talked to like that," Bob Campo said from behind him. "Not from a . . ." He seemed to look to the uniform then, as if in consideration of what it might mean. Then he finished what he had started: "Not from a goddamned Jap."

What happened next was talked about for the rest of that evening and on into the following week and we all knew, each of us in our own way, that with each telling and retelling we were making things worse, that we were, each time, pressing him farther down the path that he only seemed to have chosen but which we had chosen for him: that Ray Takahashi did not even pause in his step but turned as if he had been given a marching command, about face, and drove his fist into Bob Campo's jaw.

The foreman fell without a word. When Ray spoke again, it was to call down the rows to the boy, Bish Kenner. When there was no answer he said, just loud enough to be heard, "You'll want to get this man some water."

Now came the reply, a quiet voice from somewhere amidst the trees: "All right, Ray. I will."

Then he turned to the ground again where Bob Campo writhed in the dirt, clutching his stomach and breathing sharply against the dust. "It's Sergeant Takahashi," he said. Or maybe he said nothing. After all, this story was told to us by the teens on their ladders and would they not want a kind of closing statement? If we needed any proof of what he had done overseas it was there upon his uniform, the story somehow held in the shape of those three chevrons stacked one upon the other and pointing upwards on each sleeve. Sergeant Takahashi was home.

———

WHEN HE REACHED THE WILSONS' at last it was, like everything, just as his memory had preserved it and so he peopled it with the Wilsons of his memory, expecting them to appear, to greet him, smiling on his return from the war, Mr. and Mrs.

Wilson and Jimmy and Helen. But when he approached that Victorian upon its hill—white and clean and glowing amidst the green blades of the orchard trees—it was quiet and still. The curtains were open but the direction of the sun had rendered them opaque, so that when he stepped onto the porch the windows were but incandent plates of blinding light.

He might have circled to the side yard to peer up at Helen's window or, on the opposite side, to Jimmy's, but instead he went to the front door and knocked. Then waited. Then he knocked again.

He had thought, imagined, that it would be Jimmy or Mr. Wilson or even Helen who came to the door. He had not anticipated Mrs. Wilson—Evelyn was her name but Ray had only ever called her Mrs. Wilson—and so he was brought up short. Seeing her there—her thin frame, light brown hair, aquiline features, skin gone olive from the long days of summer—was still less surprising than the expression on her face, at once hard and confused and filled with some mixture of grief and rage, emotions that passed over her face as if patterns of weather, clouds of different altitude and color and consistency and threat, fog and rain and hail and high winds, so that Ray took a moment even saying her name, at last managing the four syllables, "Mrs. Wilson," and then paused as she stared at him, goggle-eyed, before adding, at last: "Is Mr. Wilson at home?"

"You," she said simply.

"It's me, Mrs. Wilson," he said, nodding. "It's Ray. Ray Takahashi."

"Ray Takahashi," she said quietly, still staring at him, her eyes flashing with an emotion he still did not recognize.

And so what he determined was that somehow, just as he

could not identify the expression on her face, he too must have remained unrecognized or unrecognizable to her, his short hair and uniform making him into a foreigner. "I was in the army," he said. He pulled his hat down from his shorn head now, holding the olive cloth in both hands before him as if something fragile. "I fought the Nazis in Europe."

"The Nazis?" she said. This a clear question.

"Yes, ma'am," Ray told her. "I just wanted to speak with Mr. Wilson. Oh, and you too of course. Are Jimmy and Helen at home?"

When she spoke at last her voice was one that Ray had never heard before, not from her or anyone: a low breathy sound as if she were just on the edge of running out of air. "You get away from me," she hissed.

He stood silent in the face of it, mouth open, hat still clenched in one hand, thumbs at the seams of his trousers.

"You get off my porch," she said now, the volume rising even as her voice trembled. "Go on! Get off my porch!"

"Mrs. Wilson?" He stepped backward as she advanced.

"I don't want you coming near this family. Do you hear me? Do you?"

"I don't understand."

"Just get away. Get away." And she was coming for him now, her hands out, open-palmed but swinging so that he had to raise his own hands to keep her from battering his face, all the while retreating down the final step and into the grass again. She did not pursue him onto the lawn but remained above him, breathing hard and fast, the image of her in the hot slanting sunlight amidst the dappled shade like some creature of myth, the avenging mother, the avenging wife, Onryō or Ame-onna or something equally terrible, and yet what did she have to avenge? Did she not recognize him? Could she not see that it was Ray, Ray who had spent nearly every day of his life in her presence, whom she had fed at her own table as many times as his own mother had fed Jimmy and Helen? And yet now there was this moment, this moment of confusion and, yes, of terror.

"Mrs. Wilson?" he cried. And then her first name, a name he had not dared call her in all the years he had known her, years which had spanned the entirety of his life, a name which he said now in a kind of desperation, for recognition, for understanding: "Evelyn."

But already she was gone, her small, thin frame rotating back to the house and swallowed by its cool darkness, the door banging shut behind her and then all the world, the grass, the sun, the orchard suspended between, fell back into silence. The soldier stood for a long while there in the yard, hoping and perhaps even expecting the door to open again, for Helen to appear or for Jimmy, his friend of all the years before, or even for Homer Wilson himself, friendly patriarch, expecting it all to be some kind of misunderstanding. But the door remained closed, the house silent, and at last he turned upon the grass and headed south again, across the lawn and into the orchard so that he could see the lit stripe of the road through the shadows of trees so heavy with plums that he might have simply reached up and plucked one down to his waiting mouth. Maybe he did just that. Or maybe he only walked on, hungry and alone and already pining for a life that he knew he could never again claim as his own.

2

I WROTE THE PRECEDING IN MAY OF 1969 WHEN I WAS twenty-one years old, thinking that it might be the start of a book, since the book I was trying to write, a book fictionalizing the year I had spent in Vietnam and which I already imagined would be something akin to Mailer's *The Naked and the Dead*, that book, my book, seemed to be washing out from under my feet with each passing day. I had managed to complete but a single, unconnected chapter since returning from Southeast Asia and had the luck—bad luck as it turned out to be—to place it in *Esquire* magazine. The editor there, Harold Hayes, somehow fished my pages from the slush pile that presumably swam across his desk with each afternoon's tide of mail and included my writing in a magazine that had published the likes of Norman Mailer, Joyce Carol Oates, John Updike, William Burroughs, Susan Sontag, Gay Talese, and so on. I felt, with all the naïveté that youth can muster, that I had already made it, that I was a full-fledged member of that exclusive, chrome-plated fraternity of writers.

But in fact the publication of that piece effectively stoppered my inkwell altogether and the big book, "The Vietnam Book," simply and resolutely refused to answer my feeble summons. Now I wonder if I was just too close to it, but at the time that very proximity felt like the stuff of great fiction, and so, upon my return, I spent many months shuffling through my various note cards, ideas, fragments, and nightmares, with an obsessiveness that sometimes terrified me. The fierce entanglement of my imagination and my memory had become a knot impossible to unravel.

I have written many novels since those days, some of which may well be good enough to be remembered, although to this day I have yet to revisit the war, my war, in any sustained piece of fiction. I have waited so long now that it sometimes feels as if my experiences in Vietnam have already been told and retold dozens of times: the mud and canals and paddies and helicopters and the unseen enemy—faceless, nameless, perhaps not even wholly human—and the booby traps and the air strikes. The basic narrative has repeated itself in films and, most importantly to me, in works of fiction and nonfiction, some penned by friends and colleagues and much of which has helped me understand what happened over there and how the heavy stone of that experience continues to ripple out over a life that has been, at times, troubled by its own hidden currents. Much of the war was simply boredom on a level that is difficult to articulate—but one does not have nightmares about six weeks of boredom but, instead, of those brief flashes of murderous combat when our tracer rounds ripped into the blue-shadowed moonlight and I used my Prick 10 to call down fire from the sky.

If the kind of experiences I had in Vietnam have already become a tired American myth, overtold, overanalyzed, then perhaps this is a good enough reason to justify what I am trying to do in these pages, returning to the 1969 of my memory not to write about Vietnam at long last but instead to narrate the story of someone I did not know but whose time in Placer County has come to feel inextricably tied to my own. That Ray Takahashi was a real person, not a product of my imagination, has complicated matters some, for much of his story is impossible to know for certain and I have indeed relied on my imagination when facts have proven inadequate to the telling of the tale. Nonetheless, I have researched with enough thoroughness to know when he exited the train and to whom he spoke and what the woman I have here called Evelyn Wilson said to him on the porch of her house when he first stood there after returning from the terror of the war in Europe.

That I did not finish the story of Ray Takahashi in 1969 or in the subsequent fourteen years to follow, that I am finishing it only now, in 1983, can be explained by several recent occurrences, not the least of which have been the deaths of the principal players in this story, especially the passing of the woman I sometimes called my aunt, although she was, in reality, a second cousin twice removed. What you will find in these pages is an attempt to re-create events that occurred primarily in the late summer and fall of 1945, the details of which I mostly understood in 1969 and which I am finally putting down on paper today.

I have seldom written so close a narrative as the one here assembled, a narrative which overlaps my own family's history. My great-grandfather, John Frazier, after whom I am named, was an early resident of Placer County, a man who was, family legend holds, the first to plant peaches here. Since then my family has scattered across the state, putting down roots in Southern California and the Bay Area and some, like my parents, remaining in Placer County although not in agriculture, my mother teaching at the old grammar school in Auburn until she had her three children, and my father, a dreamer with a head filled with plans and schemes that never came to fruition, sporadically producing amounts of cash at unpredictable intervals, mostly via the repair of household appliances.

My parents moved us all to Southern California in the early 1960s, my mother for a new teaching position and my father for a job in an assembly plant, and so by the time I was a teenager it felt like home. Nonetheless, the old memories of my early childhood in Placer County, amidst the scattered dry oak forests of Auburn and Newcastle, sometimes called to me with a strange and persistent song positively luminous with nostalgia: golden hills and ghost pines and cold clear creek water on hot summer days. The place felt, to my memory, too perfect somehow, too vigorous in its beauty and innocence, and so, when I returned to Alhambra after the war to discover that I simply could not reenter the old routines nor offer myself up to the judgment of my parents, both hawks who could not, despite their care for me, separate their politics from the grim reality that sat before them at the kitchen table, I began once again to ponder my quiet childhood memories of Placer County. It was but a day's bus ride up the interstate from my then–Southern California locale.

The larger and perhaps more immediate problem was the dope habit I had developed overseas, a habit I was desperate to hide from my parents and from myself and which may have placed as much stress on them as it did on me, as they likely had no idea why I swung between being utterly out of my mind with nervous fear and nodding off to a furtive, exhausted sleep. What I wanted more than anything was to be somewhere that felt safe and from which I might isolate myself and my demons and try to scramble up out of the cloud of white vinegar-tinged smoke that seemed to wrap itself around me like a snake, this while the dull reverberations of *The Huntley-Brinkley Report* murmured through the bedroom wall from Channel 4. Good night, David; good night, Chet.

Were it not for my grandmother's kindness, I have no idea what might have happened to me. It is not inconceivable to imagine myself dead somewhere or destitute and sleeping under a bridge. When she answered the door of her quiet Newcastle home upon my arrival, it was immediately clear that my letter to her had not arrived—as it turned out it never would arrive— and yet her face beamed with happiness as I stood on the porch. How this woman of goodness and grace had given birth to my own mother, a stern and earnest grammarian and taskmaster whose values boiled the entire world down to a strict equation of right and wrong, has never become clear to me. Perhaps my father's own sense of rigid moral clarity changed my mother somehow. In any case, my grandmother's smile and her tears brought on my own as she pulled me into the shade of her little living room and sat me down and handed me, of all things, a cup of tea and a stale cookie. "You're home now, John," she told me. I asked her if I could stay for a few days, just a few days, and she told me what I knew I would hear, that I could stay just as long as I wanted. Those words made me break down all over again and she patted my back, repeating, "You're home now," and "You're safe now," and "Everything's going to be just fine," so many times that I almost came to believe her.

Over the next few days I managed to get through the worst of the sickness that comes with sobriety, that razor-backed horror washing over me with no one around to help but my grandmother, a woman who presumably thought I had brought some fatal illness back from the jungles of Vietnam and who summoned the town's doctor to my bedside, his face, in the fever dream of my hallucinating mind, shaking to pieces each time I looked at him. But that terror dissipated. Maybe I healed in the end. Such things are difficult to pinpoint when you are taking inventory of your own heart.

The moment I was able, I set up my battered typewriter on a small table under the window in the closet-like spare bedroom of my grandmother's house, a tiny but charming single-story Victorian sandwiched between two similar homes near the center of what had, perhaps, once constituted the town, although the freeway had done away with much of its small bustling life by the time I came to live there. From my grandmother's front porch, I had opportunity to watch the sporadic passing of those few remaining citizens across what seemed the town's central square. It was, even to my cynical gaze, the kind of life one might have seen in a movie from the preceding era. The view from my grandmother's porch was of a vacant lot, recently paved, lined on the side opposite by a long low building, its slanting roof the color of very old rust. My grandmother told me it had been a fruit-packing shed, a railroad spur apparently having once sidled directly up to its broad, open doors. Why there was no evidence of this industry today I did not ask, for at the time the local color mattered to me only in that it was not the darkening twilight shadow of the mangrove-choked rivers of the Rung Sat, where my division had stalked the jungles in search of the invisible enemy and to which I still returned almost every night, the forest more nightmarish even than the reality had been, the thatched-roof homes ever-ablaze. It is not an exaggeration to suggest that America had become, to me and maybe to every soldier returning to its soil from Southeast Asia, an alien place, as if the men and women I saw from my grandmother's porch were simply acting out a role given them by someone else, sent to wander in limitless and ignorant bliss in the clean white avenues of a clean white America. That this world and the world from which I had come could both exist simultaneously and without apparent contradiction was a fact that I could not reconcile.

My grandmother was a quiet woman accustomed to her own routines, and so when I was not staring at a blank sheet of paper and failing to type the sentences I still hoped would help me make sense of where I had been and what I had done, there was little to occupy my time. Many days I would spend wandering up and down the country lanes on foot, my only aim being to fill the hours, and this was how I stumbled into my first postwar job.

Across the freeway to the east, the ridge turned in a kind of bulb that was known—according to my grandmother—by the absurdly genteel name of Chantry Hill, at the base of which stood a tiny cinder-block filling station. The station looked dark and cool and had a Coca-Cola machine out front, and one hot summer afternoon I found myself afoot, rummaging in my pockets for the necessary dime and then watching the bottle roll down its metal ramp until it lay cold and wet in my hand. It was then that I saw the HELP WANTED sign in the window.

"Hot enough?" In the shadowed doorway stood a balding, middle-aged man in a sweated-through white shirt.

"Sure is," I said in response, levering the bottle cap off with the opener screwed into the side of the machine.

The man introduced himself in a way that was meant to elicit some information and, because I could think of no reason not to, I told him about my grandmother and indicated roughly where she lived, thumbing over my shoulder toward town.

"You a vet?"

"A what?"

"A veteran."

I had heard the question the first time but I could not understand why he would ask me such a thing, although after a moment I indicated that I was.

"Thought so," he said.

"Why's that?"

He gestured to my hat, which, of course, I had forgotten about: an olive-green floppy-brimmed boonie that I had worn in-country whenever I was not out actively humping the bush in my brain-baking helmet.

I was relieved that he asked nothing further about my military service, although his next question, if I was looking for work, surprised me all the same.

I must have taken a long moment before answering because he began on a long line about how the younger generation, by which he seemed to mean people younger than me, although as I have said I was but twenty-one at the time, had little respect and no sense of work ethic and so on. It was a line I had heard in various forms many times from my father, and yet something about this man's earnestness and his willingness to hire me made me ask him about the pay (marginal at best) and responsibilities (slightly less marginal than the pay) and soon enough I had been hired.

The filling station was to become my lifeline that summer. There was, of course, a period of adjustment—trying to reset my sleep rhythms so that I rose before eleven o'clock—but I managed. Each morning my grandmother would tell me to have a wonderful day and I would tell her the same and then I would push out into the bright cool crisp air, the repurposed fruit sheds silent and closed and locked, the lot between empty of cars, the whole town quiet but for the hiss of occasional traffic passing on the freeway. A quick slope downhill as the road curved past the bank and the post office and ran alongside one of the town's last surviving Victorian mansions, a tall, stately affair situated on the corner of the old highway and the edge of the interstate overpass. Sometimes I would stop on that overpass and watch the cars whiz underneath me on their way to Sacramento and on to San Francisco. Sometimes I wanted nothing more than to walk down to the on-ramp and stick my thumb out and to hitch a ride to the Haight, but although I came close to doing just that many times I never did.

My aunt's appearance came just a few weeks thereafter. I had been reading William Styron's *The Confessions of Nat Turner* that summer, my pencil periodically underlining or making a check-mark or scribbling, almost unconsciously, some note in the margins, Styron's prose so enrapturing that I almost did not even look up when I heard the car roll to a stop beside the pumps.

The truth was that I had more or less forgotten that I had any relations left in the area apart from my grandmother, and so when I saw the woman through the open window of the car I did not, at first, realize who she was. We chatted briefly as I began the process of filling the tank of her Pontiac. She was perhaps a decade younger than my grandmother—mid-sixties, if my guess was right—and seemed, even via my limited view through the window, to be more fashionably arrayed than I might have expected given the town's size and relative isolation. Her hair was covered by a thin veil of light blue and her eyes were hidden behind sunglasses that in those days still seemed exotic. Indeed, had it not been for the modest automobile I might have wondered if I was indeed catching sight of some film star of another era swung off the freeway for a tank of gasoline, an idea that seemed bolstered by her very familiarity. But then I realized that my memory of that face came not from the silver screen but from my own childhood, and before I could stop myself, I said the name by which I remembered her: "Aunt Evelyn?"

I had finished refilling the Pontiac and stood by the window now. Her face was tilted toward me, those great sunglasses vaguely insectoid. "You must have me confused with someone else," she said simply.

I might have excused myself then, getting her change from inside and letting her drive off and returning to my book, but for some reason I told her my name and then my grandmother's name.

"Oh my," she said. "You're Cousin Jenny's grandson?"

I nodded as she removed her sunglasses. The face behind them was older than my memory but just as strikingly beautiful: thin and finely featured, her nose aquiline and her eyes light blue as if lurking in her genealogy was some distant Scandinavian ancestry.

She asked if my parents had moved back to the area and when I told her they had not she seemed somehow relieved. "You're staying where?"

"At my grandmother's," I told her.

"Ah," she said. "Well, nice to see you. Let's have you and your grandmother over sometime."

"Great," I said, unhappy now that I had identified myself at all, for I had no interest in such a visit.

A few more words and then she pulled away and I returned to the shadowed interior of the office, mopping my sweating face before settling into my chair once more. Through the window I watched the Pontiac cross over the freeway, turning north before that big Victorian that marked the edge of town. The bumper of the car flashed once just as it disappeared into the high shadow of the fruit sheds, a bright blooming of sunlight reflecting across the open space under which the freeway sped unceasingly. Then she was gone, that apparition of my own lost childhood, and I was once again alone with Nat Turner and the growing rage of his troubled mind.

———

I HAVE SINCE PONDERED that moment in great detail, for had I said nothing to her, had I simply filled the tank of the Pontiac and let her drive away, I would never have stumbled into the story of Ray Takahashi and his ghost would never have come to ride upon my heart the way it has. In 1969 I only managed to write that single chapter, but my failure to continue his story was not because it had lost its hold on my imagination but instead because I could not see my way around writing about Evelyn Wilson and Kimiko Takahashi and the rest of them, not while they were still alive and their stories still belonged to them, although it is easy enough to see the opposite of that point of view, that they deserved—especially my Aunt Evelyn, or rather the woman I am calling Evelyn Wilson in this book —to see the bare, bold truth printed in black permanent ink.

And yet I have also come to understand that this story is not only a tragedy but a love story, not only Ray Takahashi's but Evelyn Wilson's too, who looked upon a child and felt within her some upwelling of emotion so surprising that she could hardly bear to breathe and yet still turned away, leaving that child in Seattle as if to leave him were to eradicate a whole swath of her history, not only from her own memory but from the memory of her family and perhaps even the town. No one yet knew the full story of what had happened—not even Evelyn Wilson herself and certainly not any of the Takahashi family—but she ensured that its pale phantom would never rise to haunt whatever sunlit days remained. And for two and a half decades it had worked, not only for my aunt but for the whole town, a place that believed in its own noble sacrifice with such fervor that its very history was made to serve that definition, certain facts remembered and others conveniently forgotten. Of the buses and the camps which are a fair part of the story to come: I do not recall ever hearing about them when I was growing up, not in school and not at home. We did not talk of what happened, of what we did, nor did we talk of the families who were taken away and who, with rare exception, chose not to return to Placer County. We banished them so completely that after a time they did not even come to our thoughts, not to the thoughts of the generations who had witnessed and experienced that removal and so not to their children's. So it had been as easy for this place to forget Ray Takahashi as it had been to forget his family, his return only a lapse of a few weeks, his absence a kind of relief for our collective conscience. They were gone. That was all. They were gone by way of Executive Order 9066 and yet that order was only the most recent manifestation of a general feeling of difference and separateness held within.

Even after everything that happened, there is no doubt in my mind that Mrs. Wilson would not have approved of me writing this book, despite my having gone through the usual efforts to obfuscate the facts while still keeping an eye on the truth: changing the names and a few pertinent details until no one can be blamed but me. The two of them are unlikely protagonists, she and Kimiko Takahashi, their coming together, once I understood it, seeming nearly impossible—that Evelyn Wilson would, two and a half decades after the war, in the era of Vietnam and in the terrible wake of the assassinations of Martin Luther King Jr. and Robert Kennedy and when she must have felt as if the very fabric of her country was coming apart at the seams, that she would return to Kimiko Takahashi's side as if connected by some great and invisible thread, unbottling not only her own terrible history but the terrible history of the town itself. It hardly seems possible and yet so much had aligned: that I would be in the town at all, that I would be working that day at the filling station (or that I would even have a job at a filling station) and that the woman I knew or had once known as my Aunt Evelyn would arrive to fill up her Pontiac just at the right moment. She must already have been pondering how to get from Newcastle to San Jose and then came upon me as if by providence, something I did not yet know or understand until a few days later when a knock came upon my grandmother's door.

I was at my desk, staring at my increasingly dusty and disused typewriter next to which rested a small stack of note cards covered by a nearly incomprehensible cramped script which constituted what I still hoped would become my book. I heard first the murmur of my grandmother's voice and then another voice which I did not recognize.

I had no intention of stepping out of that room, assuming that the visitor was one of my grandmother's friends, for the front room of the house was, in the afternoons, something of a meeting ground for Newcastle's septuagenarian and octogenarian set. So I was surprised when my grandmother's pale, thin knuckles rapped gently on my door and her dry voice called my name.

The visitor, of course, was Evelyn Wilson. I was surprised to see her because I had assumed that her comment about having my grandmother and me over to her home was a kind of polite dismissal. I did not know the woman, after all, despite being in some very distant way related to her, the lines of connection so thin and stretched that it was unclear where they met, if at all. And yet here she was in my grandmother's living room, seated on the little settee near the window, her knees close together and her handbag on the floor next to her feet. She rose when I entered the room and said my name and then extended her hand—palm down—which I took and did not know what to do with and shook awkwardly and dropped again. She smiled and nodded and for a moment we simply stood there, facing each other like shy awkward partners at some high school dance, until she told me, kindly but firmly, to sit.

"I'm sorry if I seemed distracted at the filling station."

"Oh," I said, "no, I didn't think that at all. That you were distracted, I mean."

"I was just surprised to see you. That's all."

"Sure," I said.

"I won't keep you," she said. "I just came by to ask a favor."

My grandmother had entered the kitchen and returned now with a tray upon which rested a small teapot and a plate of sugar cookies. Where the latter had come from I did not know for I surely would have eaten the entire package had I come across them during one of my forays into the cupboards. She entered the conversation now, and so it turned to news of Evelyn Wilson's family and my own, that my parents were living in Southern California and that she, Mrs. Wilson, lived alone, her husband having suffered a fatal heart attack several years before.

"That must be very difficult," my grandmother said to her.

"As you know, Jenny," she said, "you get accustomed to it in time."

I had stopped wondering what favor Evelyn Wilson had been preparing to ask me, thinking that it must certainly be something very minor, like cutting her grass or doing some small repair to her home, or even taking a look at her Pontiac, since she had seen me employed at the filling station and might then assume, erroneously, that I knew something about the workings of automobiles. Her question, when it finally came, indeed seemed connected with just such an assumption, asking me, apropos of nothing, if I was a good driver, to which I replied that I supposed myself good enough.

"I wondered if you'd do me a great favor," she said then. "I have to meet someone in San Jose. I was hoping you might drive me."

"To San Jose?"

"My eyes just aren't what they used to be," she said.

I did not respond at first, if only because I was confused by the request; driving a distant relation I hardly knew to a town that must have been something like two and a half hours away was a significantly greater time commitment than I had anticipated. Not that I was particularly occupied with anything meaningful, although of course I still labored under the misguided impression that my book project was well under way.

"I'm sure he'd be glad to, Evelyn," my grandmother said then.

I was caught now, of course, and so I could only parrot her sentiment. "Sure," I said. "Sure I'd be glad to help."

———

WHEN I ASKED MRS. WILSON—I had determined to call her Mrs. Wilson now rather than Aunt Evelyn, as she was not technically my aunt and calling such a woman by her first name seemed impossible to me at that time—where exactly we were headed, she would only tell me that she was going to visit someone or that she was going to meet someone and when she seemed reticent to offer any additional information I let it drop. Much of the remainder of the drive was accomplished in silence, something of a surprise since I had assumed, for no reason other than my previous experiences in conversation with those I perceived of as *adults*, that I would be subjected to some manner of questioning as to my own life and my own decisions. But Mrs. Wilson said almost nothing, the most significant exchange of what was nearly six hours in the car, round trip, being a moment in which she asked if I was driving as fast as I felt comfortable.

"I can slow down," I told her.

"No, no," she said in response. "I thought you might go a bit faster is all."

And so I did, speeding west along the interstate in the early morning, the freeway descending the hills and then burning in a ruler line across the Central Valley before shifting, just after the golden hills beyond, to run south along the edge of the bay. We caught occasional glimpses of the ocean and the bridge, small pleasure craft with their shining white triangles of sail taut against the endless oceanic breeze, and, beyond them, lumbering barges heading into the Port of San Francisco, its shape that of a ghost city rising from a dark gray ribbon of fog lined, on its top edge, with a stripe of pure white light that reminded me, yet again, of the smoke of my addiction. I knew I could score in that great gray metropolis and the thought of that possibility bade me break into an anticipatory full-body sweat.

Mrs. Wilson had removed a small map from her purse at some point and now directed the car off the interstate and then down one street and another, the Pontiac's great pale blue hood jutting out ahead of us like a diving board. I still did not even know if we were looking for a business or a private home, so when she at last told me to pull the car to the curb I was not sure if we had reached our destination or if she was only pausing to gather her bearings, until she told me to shut off the ignition. She turned the mirror toward her own face and spent a moment looking herself over before asking me first for the car keys (which she slipped into her handbag) and then if I would come with her.

She did not wait for my answer, and yet a moment later I stood beside her on the sidewalk, staring at the house in front of which I had parked the Pontiac. It was utterly unremarkable, yellow, with a small white porch in the front framed by thick, square pillars, a house in a style still known as a California bungalow. I did not know Mrs. Wilson well at that time— I have come to the conclusion in the years since that no one really knew Mrs. Wilson particularly well—but even a complete stranger would have sensed her distress in that moment, the way in which she seemed to gather herself, to untangle herself, waiting there on the street outside that house until I finally asked her if she needed some assistance.

But then I saw her, the woman who had captured Mrs. Wilson's attention so completely, a woman who stood on the porch of that yellow bungalow, her face and shoulders yet in shadows so that I could not make out her features. Mrs. Wilson did not answer me and did not move until my hand came up, tentatively, to her elbow, grasping it gently, feeling the thin bones of her arm beneath my grip. Only then did she step forward at last, moving toward the house, the figure there continuing to watch us approach without movement or comment until she, Mrs. Wilson, finally stopped at the base of the concrete steps that led to the house's landing.

"Kim?" she said. "Do you remember me?"

The woman there looked down at us, her face—I saw now that she was Asian, not Vietnamese but certainly Asian—betraying nothing, no sign of recognition or even of acknowledgment.

"I guess you're wondering why I'm here," Mrs. Wilson said then.

"Who's that?" the woman on the porch said.

Mrs. Wilson looked at me and by the expression upon her face I knew that she was momentarily surprised to find me there. "Oh," she said, "this is my cousin's son. John. He drove me."

"Hello," I said lamely.

The woman on the porch nodded. She was, I could see now, Mrs. Wilson's age or close to it and was dressed more casually than my aunt, in a simple blouse and slacks, her black hair spun up about her head like cotton candy, a style almost identical to my aunt's but for the absence of a head scarf.

For a moment I thought she might simply dismiss us by returning to the interior of that little house but at last she nodded. "Mrs. Wilson," she said quietly, as if confirming to herself that this was who stood before her. "You had better come inside."

3

MY AUNT INTRODUCED THE WOMAN AS MRS. TAKAHASHI. I would come to understand only later just how entangled the two women were, a red thread tying together not only their own lives and their husbands' lives and the lives of their children but pulling a taut line across history itself. And yet only in hindsight does it feel like fate, like providence, the initial connection between them, between their families, not brokered by the women at all but by their husbands and even that a kind of coincidence made meaningful only by our viewing it as a past event with everything else strewn out beyond it—all the pain and heartbreak and yes even death—so that the very coincidence of their meeting feels, in the end, less like coincidence and more like synchronicity. And yet how easily could Homer Wilson have kept his mouth closed in his frustration and, even if he did speak, how easily could Kimiko Takahashi have ignored those English words, instead continuing to walk behind her husband in the dust and slow heat of the afternoon.

I heard the story many years later, in the days after Mrs. Takahashi's funeral when I sat with her adult daughters, Doris and Mary, and told them everything I had learned about their family and about my own, and they told me what I did not yet know, the story of that initial meeting under the shade of Homer Wilson's failing peach trees, and not only that but the story too of the years that had come before, all the way back to Japan. That first story had come at some remove, the narrative of their lives in Newcastle only spoken in the house when they had been children, for the Wilsons were not discussed in the Takahashi home, not after Tule Lake and Jerome and Oakland and San Jose. That was a past, a betrayal, to be erased from their minds.

In the fable I was told, the year was 1923 and Hiro Takahashi must have felt that his dream of a new life in America had been an illusion, its shape blowing away like the thin road dust that rose in pale eddies around their feet: his own and those of his young wife, infant child in her arms. He had been working for a variety of ranches and orchards and the constant scrambling from one to the next had run him down to a thin hard wire of worry and fatigue. Now that his young wife held a child to her breast that worry had become a kind of fever.

So consumed was Hiro in his own thoughts that he did not even hear the voice that came from the peach trees that lined the road: "Goddammit all to hell!" It was Kimiko who reached forward and touched her husband's arm and told him, in quiet Japanese, to wait. "Chotto matte yo," she whispered.

Hiro stopped and looked about him as if waking from a dream. Trees. The road. And Kimiko with the baby in her arms. Looking at her there, glowing in the sunlight, it is not hard to imagine that, for all his exhaustion, he might yet have felt all his labor worthwhile. His grown daughters would tell me that he often spoke of Kimiko with a kind of awe, as if, even after all their lives together, he still could not believe that she was his, that she remained by his side through all their years of struggle, his constant failure to establish himself in a country he had assumed, back when he had still lived under the protection of his family in Yamanashi Prefecture, would provide him with opportunities that his home simply did not, especially after his eldest brother had married, and thereby laid official claim to the orchard that had been in the Takahashi family for generations, an event that starkly defined what he had always known, that the family orchard would never be his.

His initial response had been to try to make a new start in the city of Kōfu, a few hours' walk from the grapes and peaches that had been his life's work, and although he found employment quickly—washing dishes in a rooming house—he knew with immediate certainty that there was nothing for him in the city. On moonlit nights he would sit and stare out at the blanched peak of Mount Fuji, knowing that, despite everything, it was the same mountain he had been staring at since he was a boy working among the trees and vines of his father's orchard. Even there in Kōfu, sitting in the lantern-lit darkness, it felt as if he could almost reach back into his own past to claim it as his own, but instead there was only the city all around him encased in shadows and the pale eternal shape of the mountain, blue and faintly luminous against the black sky.

His father had been to America once, had worked there when he was a young man, and this was where the idea must have come from. There was nothing for him in Yamanashi Prefecture, not in the countryside and not in the city, and so one afternoon he returned home to the family orchard in the shadow of Fujisan, paid his respects to his father and mother and to his oldest brother and his brother's pregnant wife and mother-in-law too, and then disappeared across the wide endless Pacific. He had told them he would return once he had earned some money, a kind of nest egg, but in truth he knew he would never see his family again. Sometimes, when the moon shone full upon the orchards of Placer County, he could be found wandering the high hills, staring out toward the west, out across the valley and perhaps, too, across the sea to where Mount Fuji still stands watch over the orchard of his childhood. Maybe such things really happened or maybe they are only part of the narrative I have built for him, for myself. He would never see Fujisan again either.

His brother's marriage had pushed him away and yet it was his brother who also provided his salvation. Hiro was employed in Vacaville by then, picking fruit for a stern Japanese farmer ten years his senior, and when his brother's letter arrived Hiro was excited to hear news of home. But there was something else in the small envelope as well: wrapped in the letter's paper was a photograph of a young woman, a girl really, in a traditional kimono, her hair swept up in a style that so reminded him of his home that he nearly shouted with longing. He supposed she was attractive, although he also knew that such a thing hardly mattered. Powdered face and black eyes. The letter offered sparse details: Hiro's parents and brother had arranged the match with help from a nakōdo. The woman came, the letter continued, from a family of good standing in Tokyo. It did not occur to him to question the specifics: the unlikeliness that a city girl from a good family would needs be shipped off to marry a farmworker in California. What he wondered instead was if she would be able to adapt to the life he had in America, although he knew too that it had been the matchmaker's job to determine the answer to this question and many others as well. He knew very little, the fairer sex yet a mystery to him, and he could hardly fathom the notion that this woman, Kimiko, whose photograph he carried in his shirt pocket, was to be his own.

When she arrived in Vacaville early in the fall of 1920, he had moved to Loomis and then Penryn, and she followed. By the time I returned to Placer County in 1969, these towns were little more than brief off-ramps from the roaring freeway that passed from San Francisco to Sacramento to Lake Tahoe and beyond, but then they were bustling hamlets, each with its own identity and purpose, and Newcastle yet among them. Hiro had come north-east on the word of a man he had met at the Vacaville Buddhist Church, following that man's word only because he felt, in his heart, that he was not meant to be a laborer all his life but that there had to be something more to the years that would follow than working some other man's plot of land.

She joined him in Loomis. They lived, those first years, in a building that was not much more than a shack in a row of similar shacks occupied by similar people—young couples and some bachelors, some even with elders or with children. When he was moved to the internment camps at Tule Lake and later Jerome in distant Arkansas, it would often come to him that his shelter in the camps was still better than it had been during the first few years of his marriage, Kimiko bearing his first child in a room six feet wide and ten long. They named the child Raymond, a name Hiro had seen in an American magazine.

The year was 1923 then. Hiro was twenty-two years old; Kimiko had just turned twenty.

It was soon after the birth of their first child that the voice had come from the orchard rows and Kimiko had stopped her husband with her hand, with her gentle words. Hiro was just preparing to ask her what was wrong when the voice came again—"Shit, shit, shit!"—and this time Hiro heard it himself, looking for a moment to his wife and the baby she held in her arms, and then stepping from the swirling eddies of dust and into the grass between the trees: "Hello?" he called in English. "Do you require help?"

There was at first no answer from the trees and so Hiro called again and now a voice returned—"Who's there?"—and Hiro continued forward, calling his own name in American order, his given name first and then the family name: "Hiroshi Takahashi." It was spring and the trees should have been bursting with new buds and many were, but here and there in the branches were leaves curled and blistered in bright orange and red as if pustules filled with blood. Hiro repeated his call, "Do you require help?"

And then there he was: a young white man, about his own age, straw hat partially obscuring his face so that Hiro could not see him fully until he tilted his head back to return Hiro's gaze. A freckled nose. Ears larger than one might expect and canted in Hiro's direction as if he were a horse and had swiveled his ears forward to better hear the man who stood before him. "Ah hell," he said, clearly embarrassed, "I don't know what I'm doing."

"I hear from road," Hiro said.

"Yeah, I'm just throwing a tantrum all by myself." His hair was light brown, not quite the yellow of some of the hakujin but close. They both wore denim bib overalls, faded to a nearly identical hue.

"Tantrum?" he said now, a faint smile on his lips.

"Angry at myself for not spraying when I should've," the young man said.

"Peach leaf curl," Hiro said simply.

"Peach leaf curl," the young man repeated. Then he looked up. "Bordeaux I guess," he said.

"No," Hiro said. "Lime sulfur."

"That so?"

"Hai," Hiro said. Then he repeated the word in English. "Yes. Lime sulfur better."

"What's your recipe?"

"Two-thirds to one-third," Hiro said.

"Two-thirds being the sulfur."

He nodded. "Ground like salt," he said. "Very fine. For winter and maybe February." This latter English word, *February*, was difficult to say and he felt his mouth slipping over the word as he struggled with it.

"Yeah," the man said now, "for some reason I never got around to it. Jesus there's just so much to keep ahold of. Maybe I can prune this back?"

"No pruning now," Hiro said. "Too late."

"Yeah I guess I know that too." He paused and then said, "You're . . . what? Chinese?" The man had been looking from Hiro to the fruit and back again but now he stopped and really looked at the man before him, a face deeply tan, eyes dark but sparkling, cheeks slightly drawn, not from privation but from, the young man thought, a kind of strength. He was taut as a bow. That much was clear just from looking at him.

"Japanese," Hiro said. "Late for lime sulfur but maybe try. Paint on here and here and here." He pointed to the trunks, their shapes unpainted, unmarked by the whitewash of the sulfur. "Start process."

"Start what now?"

Hiro paused, thought hard about the English *r* sound, and then said carefully, "Process."

"Ah yeah. *Process*," the young man said. "Sorry." Then he said his name: "Homer Wilson."

"Hiroshi Takahashi."

They shook hands, and for a moment Hiro stood there in the shade next to this man, this Homer Wilson. If he felt something of the magnetic pull that would draw the two families together he did not show it, and yet it had to be there, a pull of such force that it would draw them together even long after history had blown them apart.

At last Hiro nodded. "Have a nice day," he said. Then he turned back to where he had left his wife and baby in the road.

"Ah wait wait," the man said. "You working around here?"

Hiro told him for whom he had worked and that he was looking for something more permanent, somewhere he might stay, adding, after some discussion, that he had a new baby and that it was hard on his wife to be on the move all the time.

"Seems like you know about trees," Homer said then.

"Yes," Hiro answered. "Family orchard in Japan. Peaches and Kyoho."

"What's that?"

"Ah, grapes. Like . . . ah . . . Concord."

The man nodded in a kind of low arc, as if he were scooping up a pail of water with his mind, the ears waving in the air like the empty husks of melons. "I could use some help," he said now. "Maybe you can help me with your recipe. The lime sulfur, I mean."

Hiro looked at him. "A job?"

"I can't promise much," the man, Homer, said, "but if you can help me get these trees in some kind of order we can work something out. For the pay I mean. Maybe we can figure out a way to hold back the curl at least."

"No place to live."

"Oh I can take care of that," Homer said. "There's a little cabin. It'll take some work. Maybe a roof. And a good cleaning."

"Me and wife and baby?"

"Of course." He paused and then said, "How old?"

"Twenty-two."

"No," the man said, smiling now. "I mean the baby."

"Ah," Hiro said. He too smiled. "Raymond. Two month." Then he stopped and said the last word again, the correcting *s* louder than the word itself: "Months."

The young man nodded. "Raymond, huh?"

Hiro nodded. "Ray."

"Good name, Ray. My uncle's name."

"American name."

"That it is," the man said. "Ours is about the same age, actually. James Herbert Wilson. We call him Jimmy." He paused, as if in thought. Then he said, "You said your name was Hiroshi?"

"Yes, Hiroshi. Short is Hiro."

"Hero?" Homer said, and so Hiro repeated it once more, pronouncing it not in the way the white man had but in the Japanese way, and to his surprise, this man, this Homer Wilson, said it back to him in much the same accent, his tongue striking just at the *r* so that the sound was nearly inaudible.

"Very good," Hiro told him. "You could speak Japanese."

"Maybe you can teach me," Homer said, smiling. "That would be a thing to know, wouldn't it? Me speaking Japanese." He laughed then; his eyes returned to the tree and Hiro followed his gaze into the branches. The sun was up there, its light shaped green, shifting as the leaves wound along the tangle of branches. Komorebi.

———

THEY MIXED THE LIME SULFUR in a huge iron kettle that had been held in Homer Wilson's shed for exactly that purpose and set it on an open bonfire they had gathered from the previous year's pruning, the kerosene flashing up like a brief impossible star and then the dry foliage curling in the heat and, after many hours, the liquid in the great cauldron began, at last, to boil. The two women, Kimiko and Evelyn, watched from a distance for a time until the sulfur's acrid reek stung the air so strongly that they were forced to retreat to their separate lives. Hiro and Homer watched them as they disappeared into the trees.

For the rest of that week, the men painted the tree trunks, working side by side and finding that there was a rhythm in the work, an ease that neither had expected. Hiro had labored, already, for a half dozen men on as many farms and had learned that employers were varying in their dispositions, some kindly and distant, some ever on the lookout for an imperceptible transgression, even when it was clear that most of the Japanese laborers, some as young as twelve years old, knew more about managing fruit and vegetable production than did the pale, grim owners. But it felt different here. This American, this Homer Wilson, wanted to learn, wanted to know what Hiro knew, and treated him as a kind of equal, even one night inviting the Takahashis into his home, an invitation which cemented the feelings Hiro already held for Homer Wilson, that he had found a friend.

That his wife and Homer's wife did not find themselves quite so well matched was nothing either of the men even considered. During those first weeks the two women did not exchange more than a few words, and in fact their interactions were so tenuous and guarded that it would take many years of proximity before the sum total of their conversations would fill a single page. It was not simply reticence; Kimiko was concerned about her lack of aptitude in the English language to such an extent that the vocabulary itself seemed to drain away from her each time she reached for it. Only when her two daughters spoke that language around her in a constant and unceasing flow did she finally come to feel she understood something of its logic and texture. But that was so much later, after Tule Lake and Jerome and Oakland, after the family had settled in San Jose and their lives had changed forever. As for Evelyn Wilson, she simply lacked the trust and patience and grace to help her young neighbor muddle through the basics of a new language. And yet there was, or might have been in those early days, a feeling between them that they might yet seek friendship, their minds independently searching for something to say and neither saying anything at all.

For Kimiko what began as a kind of grudging acquiescence faded until there was only the fact of her, of Mrs. Wilson, the woman who was the wife of her husband's hakujin friend. Although even this she secretly questioned, the idea that Homer Wilson thought of her husband in the same way her husband thought of Homer Wilson. Such things simply did not seem possible to her. She had come to America as a kind of package meant to satisfy a business arrangement between the nakōdo and the two families—her own and the Takahashis—and once they had bustled her onto the ship that transaction had been completed. And yet so much of that transaction had lacked the necessary propriety. She had been too young, for one. And there had been no meeting between herself and her prospective husband, so even that part of the process, the omiai, was absent. Only later did she puzzle out the dire circumstances of the whole event, that her parents must have needed her gone, that their finances must have fallen awry to such an extent that when they heard of the Takahashis' unmarried son in America they jumped at the chance to unload the financial responsibility of their only daughter before the window for sending picture brides to America was closed forever by government decree. And perhaps the Takahashis did not actually understand just how young she had been, not twenty-two or twenty-three but seventeen years old, in most ways still very much a child. Looking back at herself years later, a sepia photograph the nakōdo had sent to Hiro in America and which he would keep for all the years of his life, she was struck by just how innocent she appeared: dressed in a formal kimono, her thin, tapered fingers woven together upon her lap. She could not remember what she had felt that day in the photographer's studio, her expression utterly blank and vacant, the white face powder giving her features the appearance of a mask.

What she would remember forever were those days on board the ship. Sick for the first week and then slowly coming into some semblance of rightness, she had considered her options with a level of detail that sometimes shocked her: jumping from the deck into the roiling sea (but alas she preferred to live), disappearing into the first city the ship moored at (but she did not know how she would survive there), trying to convince the sailors to take her back to Japan (but she could only live there now in a kind of exile from her own family). In the end, she decided to at least meet this man, this Hiroshi Takahashi.

He was not as handsome as she might have hoped and was a good deal poorer than she feared. The only reason she remained by his side was that he was, she learned soon enough, kind, not only to her but to others, and something of this pulled at her heart in ways she had not anticipated or even wanted. She did not know, of course, what she would do if she were to leave his side—she knew no one in San Francisco or anywhere else on the continent—and yet for many months the idea stayed with her, not as a real possibility but at least as an option, something that provided her a kind of compass during days of struggle and privation. It was a fiction, the idea that her location was of her own choosing, but one which helped her in those early days.

When I asked my grandmother about Kimiko Takahashi, it took her a long while to even determine who it was that I was talking about, the departed Japanese-Americans so wholly forgotten that it seemed they had been scrubbed clean out of my grandmother's mind. But then something at last came to her memory, her words forming slowly as the information trickled back into whatever shallow furrows it had left behind. "Tak's wife, you mean," she told me. "Sure, Tak's wife. I don't think I knew her name. Nobody did, probably. She was just Tak's wife. That's all."

And even if they knew she was named Kim—not Kimiko to Mrs. Wilson but Kim—that was scant knowledge compared with how they knew Mrs. Wilson herself or any of the other young women, young mothers, in the countryside and in the town, orchardist's wives. In those days, days before I was born, *their* names were known. The names of their children were known. But my grandmother's knowledge of Mrs. Takahashi was not so different from the white community's knowledge of any of the Issei women. They would have known some of the men, of course, because they were actively working in the same industry in which the white farmers were working, property lines bounding property lines, fruit weighed upon the same scales and packed into the same Blue Anchor boxes. So they knew Tak and his family in the same, general way they knew the Dois and the Uyedas and the Nakaes and the Yokotes and many others too, knew them as quiet, almost silent neighbors and did not consider what that meant, exchanging a simple greeting when crossing paths but otherwise ignoring their presence altogether.

But it would turn out that Mrs. Wilson, in her way, was unknown as well. And yet that had not always been the case, the people of the town and the countryside, people with whom she had grown up, speaking of her as if of two separate women, a serious but not unsmiling teen who would become a young bride and young mother and then, almost as if a switch had been flipped, the severe, unforgiving woman whom I recalled from my own childhood. That there had been another—a woman whom people had liked and not merely feared and respected—

seemed impossible to me, and yet the evidence was present in nearly every conversation I had with anyone old enough to remember who she had been in the days of her own youth. They recounted various versions of an event from which she seemed to have never fully recovered, an event that transpired one bleak, raining winter night in early 1933. Jimmy and Ray were both ten and Helen eight and Kimiko and Hiro's second child, Mary, was just shy of her second birthday, and Evelyn Wilson was nearing the full term of her third pregnancy. The Takahashis would have been awaiting the news of the birth, so when the knocking came upon their door late that winter evening, they— Kimiko and Hiro and Raymond too—would have assumed that that news had finally come, that the baby was here, that it was a boy, or it was a girl, and that all was well. But the loud frantic knocking continued. Then came a shrill child's voice from the darkness: "Help! Help!" and the door opened to reveal the boy, Jimmy, a boy who was so often at their home that the fact he had been standing outside banging on the boards instead of simply opening and entering as he had done countless times before only served, later, to underscore just how frightened he was, his panting breath steaming the air around his head. "My mama," he said. "She's dying."

4

WHAT HIRO AND KIMIKO FOUND AT THE WILSONS' STATELY
country Victorian was a scene of such heat and blood and terror that for many years to come the very memory of it would
send Kimiko's skin into gooseflesh. Homer—or perhaps it had
been Jimmy or even the little girl, Helen—had banked such
a blaze in the fireplace that the whole house steamed with
heat, the interior awash with flickering orange light as if the
furniture—sofas and cabinets and the like—were all aflame,
even as the slow patter of drizzling rain drummed against the
window glass. The little girl hunkered away from them as they
came through the door. Homer too stared at them uncompre-
hendingly at first, wide-eyed and raking his hands through his
sweat-slicked hair. When the light of recognition came it was as
if he were awakening from a dream. "Ah God, Tak," he said at
last, his hands on his friend's shoulders and his voice quavering
in panic. "You've got to do something. Please. You've got to do
something."

Hiro asked him what was wrong but Homer could only point toward the stairs, from which, even in that moment, a guttural wail descended like a cataract. It did not sound anything like Evelyn Wilson's voice, although of course it had to be. Kimiko's heart shuddered in fear and yet when she looked back to the men they were both staring at her, at Kimiko, as if she somehow would know what needed to be done, as if her gender had given her some secret knowledge. When she spoke it was in Japanese, telling her husband that she knew nothing, that she could do nothing, that someone needed to get the doctor up here or to load Mrs. Wilson into the wagon and drive her to his home across town, Homer's eyes bouncing between them—Kimiko, then Hiro, then Kimiko again—until he could remain silent no longer. "Just help her," he said in English. "Please." When Hiro asked him if the doctor was on his way Homer could only mumble that he was going to send Jimmy, was going to but had not— he did not say why—but already Hiro had turned to the boy, telling him to fetch Ray and then to run as fast as they could, not to town, not for the doctor, but for Mrs. Matsuda, the midwife, closer by a half mile or more, almost expecting the boy to protest but instead watching as he leapt all at once for the door as if he had been waiting for just such a command, his thin small body bursting outside like a young deer and disappearing into the rain-soaked night.

With the muffled impact of the door came another gruff guttural call from upstairs, a sound that was almost a growl but which was followed by a voice that was recognizably Evelyn's, although high and agonized, this time intoning actual words: "Homer?" she called. "I need you!" Then came her husband's name again, the pain in her voice a wavering of agony and despair and exhaustion, but Homer Wilson moved not in the direction of the stairs but to Kimiko's side, his hand on her elbow. "Tasukete! Tasukete!" he said, and for a moment she merely thought that she had somehow translated his simple statement—*please help* or even *save me*, he might have said in English—into Japanese, but then he said it again and she realized that he, Homer Wilson, his eyes red-ringed and wet with the threat of tears, was speaking in her own language, leaning toward her, exhausted, terrified, entreating. She might have run in that moment, might have turned and retreated down the thin path that ran from the Victorian to their small, squat country home on the slightly lower rise of the opposite hill, but she did not, instead telling him, telling him and Homer too, in Japanese, that she would go, then mounting the dark stairs to the open doorway, where she found Mrs. Wilson staring at her from the twisted sheets of the bed. "Please get it out of me," she said then. "Oh God please get it out of me."

And yet she knew nothing of childbirth except to push and push and push, and where was Mrs. Matsuda or the hakujin's doctor, Thompson, who would come from town, where was anyone who knew anything and why was she the one who had been chosen to stand here at the base of the bed between her landlord's wife's nether parts in the blood and waters of the womb, in the terror of her screaming, the pale soft feet first and then, for a long terrible time, nothing but the pain and the pushing, the whole of that baby stuck there like a stone in a pipe, those naked parts of Evelyn Wilson not even seeming as if they were part of Mrs. Wilson's flesh at all now but instead were something freakish and alien, stretched tight and swelling forward with each great exhausted push even though, still, it was only those two tiny feet, the rest like a red tunnel fleeing into wet empty darkness. But it had to come. It had to. And so she said, "Push harder," and then said it again and again and then she was not even speaking in English anymore, that language flooding away from her so that her words were only in Japanese and at last, after how much time she did not know—a half hour, an hour, a day, a lifetime—a great tearing and the sound of liquid upon the boards and the baby, blue and twisted and silent, was there in Kimiko's hands, a limp terrible thing.

"Is it out? It is out of me?" Evelyn said from her sweat-soaked sheets.

"Eh," Kimiko said. "Kawaisōni." The child's misshapen head lolled hideously in her grasp, its lifeless body stretching toward the wet boards. She did not know how to hold it, this dead thing. Not like a child. Not like a living child at all.

"It's a boy?"

"Hai," she said.

"I knew it. Why is he so quiet?"

She answered her in Japanese again and Evelyn was silent for a long moment and then, abruptly, she began to scream, at first her husband's name and then a wordless keening that rose up into the fetid, iron-scented air like a siren, her head swinging back and forth across the twisted, sweat- and blood-soaked sheets, her mouth open in a great oval of bleak despair. And, standing between her open, bare legs: Kimiko Takahashi, her own clothes equally soaked in blood and fluid, holding the blue corpse of that baby out before her as if to pass it directly to the Amida Buddha himself and thence into the pure land beyond.

———

MY GRANDMOTHER AND THE PEOPLE I spoke to in town
would tell me that something changed in Evelyn Wilson after
that black night in which Kimiko Takahashi delivered Mrs.
Wilson's dead son into the world. The Japanese midwife, Mrs.
Matsuda, arrived a moment afterwards and thumped up the
stairs to bark at the hakujin woman in Japanese as the after-
birth came, pushing her back to the sweated-through pillow
and bringing her some kind of tea that smelled like hell itself,
bidding to her drink, but she could not or would not and finally
retched what she had managed to swallow to the floor before at
last passing into an exhausted sleep, so that her last view of that
night was of the two Japanese women standing near the doorway like specters from the land of the dead, staring back at her
as if she were soon to be among them.

The funeral was held in the little plot of land in the Catholic
section of the town cemetery, both families there, the Wilsons
and the Takahashis, and around them the members of the local
Catholic parish and an assortment of citizens from the orchards
and the town, all of them standing around that small hole in
the earth, the damp air of late February drifting in mist about
them. It was an image that would return to Kimiko's memory
at various times in her life, none more intensely than in the days
slightly less than eight years later in the wake of Pearl Harbor
when it became clear that the brightness of their lives would be
extinguished with such ferocity that it would come to feel as if
the brief respite between one kind of suffering and the next was
but a fever dream. In those winter days, the earth once again
slaked with rain, what came to mind was the image of Evelyn

Wilson's face, the gray hard intensity of her gaze as she stared down into the hole, a rigidity that was, Kimiko thought, as thin and frangible as a paper mask. She had said nothing that day, nor for many days thereafter, her lips drawn and tight even as her husband's period of mourning lessened and finally was gone, he and Hiro back to their old camaraderie out in the trees and sunlight, planting a new line of plums on the edge of the south-facing hillside. But Evelyn Wilson was much slower to recover. Perhaps she never did or had. Perhaps she never forgave any of them for what had happened to her, although of course she was cordial and friendly when their paths crossed—this was what you did, regardless if the person was friend or enemy—and this was how it would be until 1942 when the buses came and the whole Takahashi family disappeared from their lives, only Raymond returning, returning as if to wreak one final act of destruction upon her heart.

After the funeral, Evelyn Wilson held herself apart from her neighbors. Hiro and Kimiko and Homer and the children still sometimes picnicked in the orchard or on the banks of the irrigation canal or sometimes drove down to the confluence of the American River in Auburn, a moment of relief from the heat and labor of the summer, but Evelyn Wilson did not join them. She was hardly a recluse, of course, for she still went to town on occasion—to Auburn for church and to Newcastle as well—and was cordial and quietly talkative to her casual friends. But were Homer to ask her to come with him and the children and the Takahashis—to the river or for a walk through the trees—she would demur and complain of a headache and Homer would give up and wander away to meet his friends and he and the children and the Takahashis and theirs would spend a Sunday afternoon or evening together. Sometimes their outings would be as simple as driving down the ridge to the low Japantown that stood with its series of ramshackle buildings under the shade of the cottonwoods in the draw at the base of Chantry Hill, pulling the truck to a stop and the children piling out of the back and Homer treating everyone to an ice cream from Yoshida's store. He would thank the shopkeeper in Japanese, an exchange which always brought a loud peal of laughter, not only from Mr. Yoshida himself but from his wife and children too and even from Hiro and Kimiko.

And so, at least for the children, there was still a kind of gold to the place, the summer rivers clear and cold with meltwater and the oaks crackling with dry heat over days that seemed long enough to encompass lifetimes. And who is to say it would not have gone on like that forever had not history itself come to intervene, the president's voice on the radio offering a monotony of Japanese aggression? They attacked Malaya. Attacked Hong Kong. Attacked Guam. Attacked the Philippine Islands. Attacked Wake Island. Attacked Midway Island. The family listened to it huddled around their little radio in the lamplight, the speaker hissing and the woodstove ticking with heat.

"Why did they do that?" Raymond asked.

"I don't know," his father told him.

"This is bad," Kimiko said in Japanese.

"It'll be all right," Hiro said in English.

Kimiko only said her Japanese sentence again.

The attack had come on a Sunday and although the following week's church service was the same as it ever was—the chanting the same, the smell of incense, the sound of the priest's voice— it also felt as if the very air of that room had changed. In the parking lot afterwards, the men clustered with the men, the women with the women, and the talk was of what might come, the voices around Kimiko in a state of quiet panic.

—My husband says they'll come to see how Japanese we are.

—They can't do that.

—They can do what they want.

—What will they do?

—My husband says they'll have the police guard our homes.

—Guard our homes from what?

—From people.

—What people?

And then the last words before the group fell into silence, the statement so resolute that Kimiko felt it like a single needle of ice plunging into her heart:

—From Americans.

It was but a few days later, after Doris and Mary had gone to school and Raymond was out with his father in the orchard, that Kimiko burned the little Buddhist ancestor shrine Hiro had built soon after they had moved into the house, breaking its shelf from the wall with a claw hammer and then taking the individual pieces from the small cabinet one by one out into the yard where a steel barrel smoked, its open circle holding within a cradle of flame into which she slid the broken pieces of wood, stirring the fire until it twisted from the mouth of the barrel like a small bright tornado. The incense holders. A small sheet of paper containing the Seikatsu Shinjo, which Hiro had written out in English for the children to practice, beside which rested the black lacquered box containing Shinran Shonin's hymns, all of which now, piece by piece, Kimiko resigned to the fire. The various lacquered wooden stands for offerings. The red candle. The cloth burned with a ferocity that surprised her. Of the metal—the bells and lanterns and such—for these she had dug a small hole near the edge of the orchard trees where the grass was thick and she thought the pieces would not be found.

She did not burn the Buddha until after she had smashed the shrine itself and had resigned each piece to the flames. Only then did she lift Amida Nyorai from where she had set it on the kitchen counter, an image of the Buddha seated upon a lotus flower, his eyes closed, thumbs and knuckles touching gently just below the curve of the open neck of his robe. For a long while she watched that impassive face blacken in the barrel, the coal spark creeping across its features, the bright glow, and finally its disappearance into flame.

"You watch," she told her husband that night, her voice a harsh whisper which she knew, nonetheless, her children could hear. "They'll come to see what we have. They'll see we're Japanese."

"We're Americans," he said. "Our children are American."

"Their children are American," Kimiko said, pointing in the direction where, across the hill, the Wilson children slept in their upstairs bedrooms.

"Doris and Mary and Raymond are as American as they are," Hiro said.

"You're a fool," she said. "You're just an old fool."

He must have heard her, for soon thereafter the rifle disappeared and the oil and gasoline Hiro kept in the shed also vanished, presumably to the small barn at the Wilsons', so when the government officials came at last—in February, later than she had anticipated—there was nothing to find in the little house at all. And yet one of the men lifted a photograph of Hiro's parents from its hook upon the wall, the figures on the paper seeming to tremble beneath their traditional Japanese clothing. "Who's this?" one of the men asked. The hakujin men were a trio in dark suits and ties and stood in the Takahashis' tiny home without apology, gruffly opening drawers and cabinets and even peering under the floorboards and shining their electric torches into the grass and weeds. There had been a moment when one of them had stood directly upon the covered hole in which Kimiko had buried the tiny lanterns from their shrine, but he had felt nothing but the earth beneath him and had moved on.

"My parents," Hiro said simply.

"Where do they live?" one of the men asked, his voice gruff and sharp. "Japan?"

"They live in Heaven," Hiro said.

The man stood looking at him for a few moments, then glanced briefly at the photograph before returning it to its nail. It was the only item she had saved from the shrine, the only object that had not become smoke, and yet, when the man had brought it down from its nail, she wondered why she had saved anything at all.

"What's this about, gentlemen?" This from Homer Wilson, stepping through the door behind them now with his gangly limbs and buckteeth and jug-ears, his voice steady and calm and even jovial.

"Just about done here, Mr. Wilson," one of the men said.

"Well, maybe you men come over for a cup of coffee after," Homer said. "Tak, you come too."

"I don't think that's a good idea," Hiro said quietly.

"Sure it is, Tak, we'll just sit and have a coffee and then we'll let these fine folks go about their business. Whatcha think, gents? Cuppa joe to get you through the night?"

"I wouldn't mind," one of the men said. And another: "Me

neither." And the third: "All right, but just one. We've got a lot of houses to cover."

"Good then." He turned to Kimiko now. "Can you tell Evelyn to put on the pot?"

She almost told him no, that she would do no such thing, but his eyes spoke to her of fear, an expression that surprised her, for what could he possibly fear in this situation? The Wilsons, after all, had nothing to lose. Not a thing. At last she nodded and pushed through the door into the cool of the early evening.

She was glad to escape that close, crowded room. Behind her came the sounds of the search and Homer's absurdly affable voice murmuring through the closed door. Above her, the sky still appeared the color of daylight, but the trees all around her had already captured the coming night in their branches, their shapes darkly blue and shining with stars. She did not want to walk the path to the Wilsons' but she knew that there was purpose in it, that Homer Wilson had a plan of some kind, if only to show these men that her husband was not some radical Japanese, but then she caught sight of a shape just beyond the white sedan the men had driven to their dooryard, a figure who, as Kimiko watched, stepped out into the silver dusk.

"Mrs. Wilson," Kimiko said.

The figure said nothing, only standing there, her face shrouded in shadow. She must have followed her husband from the house but why she had not come inside with him Kimiko did not know, although of course Mrs. Wilson had never stepped foot inside the Takahashi home. Not once.

"Mr. Wilson says put on the coffee," Kimiko said quietly in careful English. "Mr. Wilson says the men will come."

And now, at last, Mrs. Wilson spoke. "The men will come?" she said.

"Yes," Kimiko told her.

"So they didn't find anything, I gather."

Kimiko said nothing, shaking her head, although she was not sure she was any more visible to Mrs. Wilson than Mrs. Wilson was visible to her. The grass around her glowed faintly in the last light, pale and shimmering.

"You managed to get everything burned up then?"

She looked up now, quickly, her eyes hard.

"Of course I saw you, Kim," she said. "You were at it for hours. It doesn't change anything, you know. They still know you're Japanese. I mean, anyone can see that." She paused, breathing, and Kimiko thought she could see the arc of a smile there in the darkness. "Well, your secret's safe with me anyway."

Kimiko watched her there, that dark shape on the edge of the trees. Later she would wish she had spat some subtle insult in the direction of that threatening shadow but in reality she said the only English word she could yet bring to mind: "Coffee." And then she turned back toward the little house, around through the side yard and to the back, and there she lowered herself to the step and lay her head in her hands and wept.

———

WHEN I RETURNED FROM DRIVING to and from San Jose that first time, I asked my grandmother about Mrs. Wilson's relationship to Kimiko Takahashi, and the memory she came to was the same memory that was held by the old postman and the woman who had worked at the fruit shed and by the elder members of the Tokutomi family I spoke to later. They all shared the same image of the same May day in 1942, the afternoon in which the buses came to take nearly half the county's occupants away, first to Tule Lake and later to other camps scattered around the country. The gravel square was busy with anticipation that day, men and women and children gathered in knots along the edge of the square, the Takahashis and the Dois and the Hatas and the Nodas and the Nishikawas and many others besides, some white landowners and townspeople among them, many more, watching at a distance as the Issei and Nisei and Sansei waited amidst the stacked bundles that constituted their lives: some combination of suitcases and rough boxes covered in cloth or paper, bundles and simple sacks that might once have contained feed corn or grain and which now, in the heat of the summer sun, contained instead the sum total of their lives, organized into low stacks in the gravel as they— all of them, white and Japanese—waited for the arrival of the buses. Across the gravel, the slab doors of the fruit sheds were open so that the dim, dusty interiors could be seen, the belts silent, the box-machines still.

The two women had not been seen together for a long while and then, suddenly it seemed, there they were, side by side in the gravel. In my imagination I place them directly in front of the little house in which, in 1969, my grandmother resided, since that is where, I have been told, the buses were loaded. But of course they might have waited elsewhere along the edges of the town square. When I think of Mrs. Wilson now I think of a stern, aging beauty, a sixty-nine-year-old widow who had become, with the passing of years, increasingly severe and unforgiving, but then she was but forty-two, perhaps no longer young but certainly not the elderly woman I knew. Her manner, when described to me by those who had known her, was not one of tragic loss but instead manifested itself as a kind of physical bearing, as if she felt she was owed respect for some activity or action unknown or misunderstood. And this would be how she was to be remembered that summer, the summer of the removal: as somehow separate, apart, maybe even aloof, as if she had known this day had been coming and now she was simply there to watch it unfold.

She stood a full head taller than Kimiko and when she spoke, her voice, Evelyn's, Mrs. Wilson's—even those I spoke to who were her contemporaries would only ever call her Mrs. Wilson, just as they would never have called Kimiko Takahashi anything at all—was a clear bright sharp sound amidst the steady murmur of more distant voices and the occasional crunch of gravel underfoot.

"It'll be fine," Mrs. Wilson was saying, as if they were merely picking up a thread of conversation that had broken off a few hours or a few days before, perhaps on the path between their two homes. "You'll see. They just need to be careful about it is all. And you'll come right back to us. I'm sure it won't be long at all."

The Japanese woman in her shadow said nothing, only nodding quietly and staring without focus toward the gravel of the square. Behind them, away from the square, stood a little row of three small Victorians at the center of which was the house I would, twenty-seven years later, occupy with my grandmother, all of them empty now as their occupants had come out onto the sidewalk to watch and quietly discuss the events of the day, the plans of the president, the war with Japan, the reports that submarines had been sighted from California beaches, and the necessity—such were the terms used—of removing the Japs from the whole of the Pacific coast. That Homer Wilson did not share such views was a surprise to the people of the town, even though they knew of his friendship with his foreman. And yet it was still a surprise to them when Homer Wilson would stand at the meetings of the Fruit Growers Association and use words like "neighbors" and "friends" and "community members" in reference to those we had sent to the camps, as if he were under some spell.

"Anyway," Mrs. Wilson continued, "Homer'll do something about it. You'll see."

Kimiko's expression was so impassive that it seemed almost as if she did not hear Mrs. Wilson speaking at all. And yet after a moment she whispered a faint reply: "Thank you, Evelyn."

Mrs. Wilson paused now, for the woman had never, in all the years they had known each other, said her first name. She had assumed that it was some kind of Japanese tradition or even a stricture and it did not please her now that such a stricture had been broken. There had been a formality between them. Why break that formality now? Why break it ever?

"I know we've had our differences," she said then, trying to choose her words with care, "but we've got to put all that behind us now." She paused a moment, searching for the right phrase. And then there it was and she said it: "I want you to know that I forgive you."

"You forgive me?" Kimiko said quietly, still gazing at the gravel, her dark, warm hair pinned up in a globe upon her head.

"Yes," Mrs. Wilson said. "It's important to move on. Don't you think so?"

"Yes," Kimiko said in response, her tone flat, colorless. "We'll move on."

This was a kind of relief. If only Kimiko Takahashi had apologized she might well have forgiven her years before, and yet she had not and so things had settled into—what?—a kind of awkward routine of avoidance. But that was over now, she supposed. "And I'll take care of things while you're gone," she said now. "You can trust me on that."

"Of course," Kimiko said.

"Well, we're neighbors, aren't we?"

"We are."

Again Kimiko's unsmiling nod. Gaman, her own mother would have called it, that quiet suffering which was, Kimiko had been taught and now knew as intimately as she knew any thing about herself, simply the way of life, so woven into its fabric that it was part of the Four Noble Truths of the Buddha, especially, she thought now, for a woman bound inextricably to the lives of men.

The families had broken into small clusters, each only a few meters from the other. Of the groups that ranged about in the gravel, some were comprised strictly of those of Japanese ancestry, others included a white man or woman or couple standing as part of the circle, the Issei and Nisei and Sansei dressed in coats and ties if men and in clean, sensible traveling clothes if women, the whites more often in overalls or work shirts or simple dresses, so it seemed some odd meeting between Asian businessmen and white farmers, a bitter and perhaps even ironic play on the reality of the scene.

She was not looking at them, though, not at the clusters of

men and women, young and old, white and Japanese, but instead
at the image of her own son, stark and bright in his button shirt
and jeans, the Wilson children—not really children anymore, in
all actuality—standing near him, the trio huddling in the same
close cabal that they had built and maintained all their lives.
In May of 1942 he was not yet twenty years old. There would
be a darkness to his nature when he returned from the war, a
darkness that I would come to imagine as a black flower blooming over him during those nights in the Vosges forest when the
blood of his friends and companions ran in streams down the
steep mud of the brush-tangled mountainsides. (Or maybe that
was how I had come to imagine myself, the black flower my
own, the sucking mud, the biting ants, the bomb craters along
the Rach Gia filling with water and with blood.)

Now he was yet only a boy, confused and conflicted, his heart
aflame for reasons his mother would not know and would not
learn of until that day when Mrs. Wilson would appear in her
life once more, and I with her, and she would understand at last
what wild beast had come to live in her son's chest. But that day
in 1942 there was only his beauty, a beauty which, his mother
knew, eclipsed that of the Wilsons' children, neither of them
possessing their mother's porcelain delicacy but instead taking
the hale blandness of their father, his jug-ears, his bucktoothed
grin, the boy, Jimmy, getting the worst of it. Many years later
she would see a caricature of that boy in the television presence
of Howdy Doody and her distress was so acute in the face of
that recognition that she fled the room in alarm while her husband and Mary and Doris—both teenagers then—watched her
retreat in fear and confusion.

Except in direct contrast with her mother, Helen was simply ordinary, her skin pale despite a lifetime in the sun, her cheeks blotchy, and her nose covered over with freckles, hair a thin yellow that, Kimiko had to admit, shone with gold threads by midsummer, but which tended to hang thin and lank upon her shoulders. Her mother had long since given up attempting to bring it into some kind of order. In truth, Kimiko was not generally particular about beauty, and certainly not when it came to the children, but something in the tableau before her had given her pause, given her, indeed, a sense that she was witnessing something that she would never see again. It was not that she anticipated in any tangible way that they would not return to Newcastle—although of course they would not –but rather that when they did return things would have changed, even if their absence was, as Hiro and Homer both seemed to believe, just a matter of a few weeks. They would have been removed as enemies of America, and what would that do to the children, who stood now in that clutch in some manner of earnest conversation, about what she could not guess?

There with them was Raymond, his skin tan from the long summer, not the bronze of Jimmy's flesh but a darker hue, oak bark or granite. His eyes, dark and slim, still glinted as he spoke, even at this distance, under the black sheen of his hair. She realized now that he was very nearly a man. In a world different from this one he might have been a film star, such was his beauty, intense and deep and with a hint of tragedy. He laughed then and she could hear it, the sound of that moment of joy, and she wondered, not for the first time, what the future would bring to that boy, to any of those children. Both boys, their whole lives set like compass arrows pointing unwaveringly toward their own tragic ends. Hardly a year for Jimmy. Three for Ray. And Helen's life blown all to pieces in the aftermath.

Kimiko wondered how long she would have to listen to Evelyn Wilson's nervous and self-involved prattle, but then Homer Wilson's voice came, a short, sonorous sound across the stacked parcels and the gravel, calling Jimmy's name. Jimmy mumbled something to his friends and then came to where Homer and Hiro stood beside another small cluster of suitcases and boxes, their sides labeled with numbers and names. Beyond them, in the gravel, Helen's and Raymond's hands touched briefly, Kimiko watching without emotion but wondering what such a thing could mean, the touch seeming tentative and awkward between them. Just children trying to say goodbye, she told herself, for what else could it have been?

The sound of the buses now. Perhaps Homer had heard it first and this was why he had called Jimmy to his side. But why Jimmy and not Helen as well? Why not both of them?

"Raymond," Hiro called now, and the boy looked up. His face was a mask of impassivity held, Kimiko thought, over a second mask of pain and fear and heartbreak. Oh my boy, she thought. Oh my beautiful boy. "Go find your sisters," Hiro called, and the boy looked from his father to the girl—woman? no still a girl—and then Helen called, "I'll help," and they turned as one, moving away.

"Here they come," Homer said. His hand was on Hiro's shoulder. "Christ, this is a mess."

"Yes," her husband said, nodding.

"A goddamned mess." And Kimiko was surprised to see that Homer's eyes were bright and shining with the threat of tears.

"We'll get this straightened out, Tak," he said now. "You'll see. Just give it a week or two."

"And we'll take care of everything while you're gone," Evelyn said from beside him. "Don't you worry."

"Mrs. Wilson," Hiro said now, turning with solemnity toward their landlord's wife and nodding and then half bowing, "you are too kind."

Doris and Mary were there now, out of breath and excited. The sound that came up the old highway was of the hard, high squeal of air brakes and then the great roar of a diesel engine pushing up the hill. "Where's Raymond?" Hiro asked them.

"Dunno," Mary said, Doris having already spun away again, the dust clouding all around her.

"Go find him," her father said.

The girl was off at a sprint and after a time the buses appeared, three of them in all, their great broad shapes turning in a slow circle around the lot and coming to a stop in a single line, the doors opening one after the other as if choreographed, the rattle of their idling diesel engines and the seep of their exhaust infusing the air with the scent and feel of pistons and gears and the slow drip of oil, and then the engines stuttered to silence. From the windows, faces peered into the bright spring sunlight. Kimiko thought she recognized some of them but there were many she did not; so they would be clambering onto a strange bus filled with strangers headed to a strange place, and this after she had left behind her home and her country and even her language to live here with a man she had not even seen before and to make a life with him as his wife, the whole size and shape of her own destiny seeming in that moment to weigh upon her heart like a great and terrible stone.

A man had come down from one of the buses—a tall, rangy hakujin in a serge suit and floppy necktie—and it was from his thin, nasal voice that their names began to fill the air. Someone was checking their luggage tags to make sure everything had been properly labeled. She had painted each of their bags with the number and their name. Raymond had returned from wherever he had gone. Mary and Doris too.

"Takahashi," the man in the suit called. He paused and then added: "Hiroshi."

"Yes," her husband said, and the whole group stepped forward as one—Takahashis and Wilsons alike—and then came the loading of the parcels and suitcases into the belly of the bus and in the next moment she stepped onto the platform and up the steps, Mary and Doris ahead of her, Raymond just behind, her husband still outside. She knew he would be talking with Homer Wilson, talking with his hakujin friend this final time, but she could not even look through the windows now. Those already on the bus were silent, but some of them watched her and the children as they came up the aisle. She and the two girls slid into an empty seat, Raymond a few seats farther up, slumping by the window that faced the Wilsons, and although his back was to her, she thought his eyes were forward rather than cast out through the dusty glass to the sunlit square beyond.

And then there was her husband, his bearing crestfallen even as Homer Wilson's voice came, muffled, from outside: "You'll be fine, Tak." Hiro came up the last of the steps and into the aisle, his eyes finding hers and then glancing about for an empty seat and sliding in just behind her, the next family already coming up the aisle, and then the next and the next. Her husband said nothing. Mary and Doris craned toward the window. "When are we going?" one of them said.

"Soon," she said.

As if in response: the roar and rattle. A cloud of diesel smoke. The scent of oil. And then the great hulk lurched forward, first to second and then a grind into third. "Here we go!" Mary shouted at the window.

The buses rumbled away. In their wake, the Wilsons continued to cluster together in the bright sunlight, watching the dispersing dust, the square about them mostly empty now, the luggage and parcels and packages gone, the people gone, a few orchardists and curious townspeople and teenagers and children meandering around the space without purpose or destination.

"Dammit all to hell," Homer Wilson muttered under his breath. "Let's get home. Let's get on home."

As for Evelyn Wilson, her thoughts were only of relief. Maybe she would be lucky and they would never return. The thought felt guilty to her but had she not earned it?

She thought she could still hear the distant whine of the buses on the air, could hear it and could hear it and then faintly and fainter still until the final gargled flatulence of the diesel engine came as the faintest whisper on the distant stretch of the curving highway. And then they were gone from her life, gone for twenty-seven years right up until the day I drove her to San Jose to look once more upon the face of Kimiko Takahashi.

5

SO IT WAS TWENTY-SEVEN YEARS LATER, TWENTY-SEVEN
years in which both women had lived totally separate from each
other, years which were, in sum, longer than those they had
shared in the quaint, quiet town in which, in 1969, I lived with
my grandmother, and while I had assumed that I was driving
my aunt to visit some old friend or associate what I was actually
met with in Mrs. Takahashi's living room was a series of awkward and confusing silences. Neither woman seemed interested
in talking to the other, a state which became apparent almost
from the very moment in which we entered Mrs. Takahashi's
home and were bidden to sit, Mrs. Wilson in the center of a
short somewhat worn sofa and Mrs. Takahashi across from her
in a wingback chair. The room was a typical middle-class living
room that might have been occupied by anyone at all, the only
indication that its occupants had emigrated from Japan being a
single print of Mount Fuji, its pyramidal shape black against a
bright orange sky. Into one of the long pauses between the two

women I told our host that I had seen the mountain once from the window of an airplane.

"Very beautiful," she said in response, unsmiling but nodding, and then, as if to change the subject: "Would you like tea?"

"Oh," I said. "Tea? I guess so. If it's not, I mean, too much trouble."

"No trouble," she said simply and then stood and moved to the doorway, pausing there long enough to glance back at my aunt upon the sagging sofa. "You as well, Mrs. Wilson?"

"All right, Kim," she said.

In the gap that followed, I watched Mrs. Wilson but she did not meet my gaze, her face tight and sharp, masklike. "I think . . . ," I began, my throat unexpectedly dry. "I think I might wait outside."

Mrs. Wilson's eyes shifted to mine in an instant. "No, no," she said, and then, in a softer register: "Please stay. Would you do that for me?"

"Sure," I said, "but it's just that you're, you know, old friends. I didn't want to . . . intrude."

"Oh you're not intruding," she said.

I thought I might receive some explanation then but when it became clear I was not immediately ready to flee the house for the sunlight of the front yard, my aunt fell once more into silence. I might have pressed her with a question or two had Mrs. Takahashi not reappeared, bearing a plastic tray upon which rested two delicate teacups and a third that was more solid in nature, ceramic and of the style one might have found at a roadside diner. Next to the cups rested a tiny ornate bowl stacked with sugar cubes and a matching pitcher of cream. We set about putting our tea together. It was a task I really did not know how to do, truth be told, and so I followed Mrs. Wilson's lead. Mrs. Takahashi had taken the heavier cup the moment she set the tray down, reserving the two more delicate vessels for Mrs. Wilson and me, as a result of which I spent the rest of my time in Mrs. Takahashi's home worrying about breaking the cup and saucer, both of which seemed so thin that even grasping the tiny handle felt a step toward disaster.

After a time, we settled again into our seats and the awkward chitchat resumed, the whole of it setting my teeth on edge as the two of them, without moving from their seats and sometimes without even speaking, circled each other like lions on the plains of the Serengeti. Why this was the case I did not know and could not even guess, nor could I even begin to understand why Mrs. Wilson had asked me to drive her all the way to San Jose to meet with a person that, at least from my point of view, she seemed to have little interest in actually speaking with.

"Is your husband well?" Mrs. Wilson said soon after we had resumed our positions in the room.

"Yes, he's fine."

"Has he retired?"

"He won't retire," Mrs. Takahashi said. "Too restless . . ."

"What's he doing, then?"

"He works in a grocery," she said.

"Grocery? Is that so?"

Mrs. Takahashi nodded resolutely but said nothing more and did not ask the same questions of Mrs. Wilson, letting the whole conversation pause yet again. If she wondered at all why my aunt had driven—or had me drive—the two hours and forty minutes it had taken us to get from Newcastle to San Jose, she gave no indication of it. She sat clutching her teacup and offering no quarter at all, not even asking what Mrs. Wilson might have wanted or why she might have come, putting even the announcement of that desire on the shoulders of the woman who had arrived in her living room, apparently unannounced.

But then something changed in the conversation, Mrs. Wilson embarking on a kind of story, a narrative about a time she had taken her daughter to Seattle, although even as she talked of it, it was difficult to unravel the point of the tale. Her daughter had been ill, it seemed, or no, not ill, perhaps pregnant. Could that have been why? Her words were coming quickly now and I realized with a start that this story was why she had come, that she needed to tell it, although I still could not understand any more than the basic outline of the narrative. There were nuns now. An orphanage perhaps. And she had signed something and the nuns had walked away and her daughter, Helen was her name, had been angry at her for all the years since. I assumed that Mrs. Takahashi could follow the story even if I could not, so it was surprising when that woman's voice began to interject through the rising desperation of Mrs. Wilson's pleading and nearly incomprehensible tale, interjections which did not grow in volume and yet seemed to increase in intensity until it was clear that Mrs. Takahashi was nearly as lost to the story's meaning as I was.

But in many ways I could also understand Mrs. Wilson's reticence to reveal exactly why she was there, not the specifics of that reticence, of course, not yet, but I knew truth's great propensity to terrorize all too well. Even when Chiggers came to visit me later neither of us could really talk about what happened to us in Vietnam and certainly could not talk about what we had done there. It must have felt the same to Mrs. Wilson.

Like me, she knew, I think, that what she had done had been wrong but, also like me, if given the opportunity she would do it all over again in precisely the same way. Only now, these years later, does it feel as if the story of Mrs. Wilson and Mrs. Takahashi has come into a kind of focus, like looking through the wrong end of a pair of binoculars, the tiny image within the circle of the lens stark and crystalline, even what I did not yet know—what no one in the town really knew—held steady in the center of that black circle, that part, the most important part, blowing everything else into char.

The Takahashis had lived all those years under a falsehood so thick that even Evelyn Wilson's arrival in San Jose was in part in answer to its shape. But of course she did not know that either. Mrs. Wilson had reached a kind of tipping point of personal desperation and loneliness that finally pushed her to the desperate act, those twenty-seven years later, of tracking down her former tenants. It was the end of a long trail of grief and guilt that had been working upon her heart for a quarter century and without which she might well have kept all of it a secret forever. But there was the date that came back around on the calendar once a year, a date seared into the flesh of her heart, January 4, a date so increasingly fraught with emotional resonance that she began to fear the turn of the year, her mood darkening the closer she came to the holidays and the anniversary of that day in 1943 in Seattle when she had handed the child to a nun and said the words that she would remember all her life—"He's yours now. Take him away"—and the nun nodding in her calm, quiet way, the papers pale and dry in her hand, and Evelyn signing them without even looking and without any sense that she had overstepped her authority at all, for was she not still the matriarch of that family? Was it not still her responsibility to make those difficult decisions?

After it was done and the papers were signed and the child, the swaddled child, was taken away, she returned to her sister's house, that small worn structure with its scrim of dark mold along the edges of its rain gutters, the forest all around so perpetually wet and dripping that the very sight of it made Evelyn's skin crawl. In her moment of extremis she had known that Dottie was the only person in the world whom she could truly trust, but now that the birthing was complete, the papers signed, the half-breed baby gone from their lives forever, she could not help but feel a gray loneliness that seemed to drip from the very trees, puddling even in the sodden light of Dottie's kitchen.

"Is it—" her sister began, and Evelyn interrupted her: "Yes, it's done."

Dottie nodded. "You want some coffee?" She stood in the doorway that led to the kitchen, her thin body wrapped in an apron, hands patting the fabric.

And then came a reaction Evelyn did not expect, her knees wobbling and her whole body seeming to drain of vitality all at once so that she had to grasp the doorframe to keep herself from crumpling to the floor.

"You come and sit," her sister was saying to her now, her hands on Evelyn's frame, her fingers seeming to hold her together.

For a long while afterwards, they sat at the kitchen table, the coffee cooling in the tiny china cups her sister had inherited from their mother, smoking cigarettes and staring out the window as a flurry of slushy snow began to clump down from the gray sky.

"It's the only way," her sister told her. "I just can't believe she did what she did. And now of all times."

"Well, it's done."

"You're a good mother," Dottie said then. "It's what a good mother would do."

Evelyn could only nod at this.

"When's she come home?"

"I don't know. A few days, I guess."

"Well, we'll get over there to see her as soon as Tom gets home. Anyway, you did the right thing. Anyone could see that."

"Why do you keep saying that?"

"Well, honey, it's just that you look so sad."

"But I'm not," Evelyn said, a sharp edge in her voice now. "I'm fine. I know I did the right thing. Helen knows it too. I think you're the one who thinks different about it."

"I don't though, Lynnie. You know I don't. I'm always on your side."

"It sure doesn't seem like it."

"Now wait a minute," her sister said. "I opened my home to you and to Helen. I've done right by you both."

"All right, all right," Evelyn said. "Fine. You've done right."

"Well, I have."

"I said all right, Dottie. Can I just sit here for a minute, please?"

They visited Helen later that evening, the hospital's halls filled with the muted confusion of murmured and indistinct conversations punctuated by muffled squeaks and clicks as if the long white spaces were filled not with human activity but with the movement and industry of insects.

Helen's room was on the second floor. Her aunt had given

the girl a few issues of *Movie Show* and *Life* and *Photoplay* and she laid one of these aside as they entered the room. Rita Hayworth sucking a soda fountain drink through a pair of straws.

"How are you feeling, honey?" Dottie asked her.

"All right," Helen said. "I'm ready to go home now."

"Is that what the doctor told you?" This from her mother.

"Not yet."

"We'll need to wait and see then," Evelyn said. "Probably tomorrow. Depends on what the doctor says."

"I want to go home, Mama."

"I know. And we will."

How haggard her daughter looked. And how young. Evelyn had been twenty-three when Jimmy was born. Twenty-five when Helen herself had come. And yet even when she had been Helen's age she did not think that she herself had been quite so fragile, not quite so childlike, not even at seventeen or eighteen. She herself had been—what was it?—more mature? Yes, more mature, and also capable of keeping her legs closed until her wedding night, vestal and intact. This last did not seem too much to ask, to keep the wandering hands of boys within certain regions of the body and to understand which actions would lead directly to the moment that had come upon her, not just Helen but Evelyn and Dottie too, upon the whole family. Shame.

"Where is he?" asked Helen.

For a long while no one spoke, both Helen and Dottie waiting for Evelyn to answer until it became clear that she would not or could not and at last it was Dottie who spoke: "He's safe as pie, honey. On his way to a new family."

"How do you know?"

"Well I just do. Don't you think so, Lynnie?"

But still Evelyn did not answer. What she wanted more than anything was for the whole thing to be over, the entire scandal intolerable, at least to her. The fact that the people in this room knew—that Helen and Dottie knew, and that the staff of the hospital knew, and the nun who picked up the child knew—this was very nearly too much to bear, the idea of it like a fire that burned from room to room, spreading no matter what she did, even after coming all this way on the train from their little town in the orchard country to this far-flung northern clime with its dripping trees and wet heavy snow that seemed to come down in great globs like phlegmy spittle.

The truth of it might never have come out had she not pressed, her daughter breaking down one afternoon in the kitchen to tell her the truth only after Evelyn sat her down and interrogated her. Still it had been, for Evelyn, a terrible surprise; she knew something was wrong with her daughter but she had thought, naïvely perhaps, that Helen was merely worried about Jimmy, the boy having signed up for the army without consulting either his mother or father and perhaps without even telling his sister about his intentions. If Jimmy knew about Helen and *this boy*—for they did not at the time know who she had been with—he did not tell anyone before he left for the Pacific. Had he been home, Evelyn knew she might have extracted the information from him, for he had always been her own, her dearest and the one closest and most open with her, this in contrast to Helen's secrecy, her apartness, her willfulness. In truth Helen knew her daughter was more like her than Jimmy would ever be.

"Lynnie?"

She spun on Dottie now, her words clipped and hard. "What is it?"

"I was only asking if you thought the baby was off with his new family already."

"How would I know?" she said.

"I'm just trying . . . ," her sister began.

"Oh I know perfectly well what you're doing," Evelyn said. "Can we just get through this? Is that too much to ask?"

"That's what we're doing," Dottie said.

"Mama?"

"What?"

"I want to see him."

"That's not possible."

"But I want to."

Now Evelyn only shook her head. A kind of static seemed to float down over the room. Beyond the open door came the sounds of the insects again: their chittering, their snapping mandibles and claws, the fluttering of membranous wings. Her heart felt high in her chest, as if floating at the base of her throat, a hard, sharp muscle, beating.

Helen had begun to weep now, a few tears and then a kind of gasp and then it was as if she had split open from the force of her grief, her body leaning forward and great hard breaths pulling between the sobs. "Mama . . . Mama . . . ," she said between, her voice high and distorted like a radio fading on the edge of transmission.

Evelyn stood watching as if from some great distance, as if the girl who lay in the hospital bed were no kin to her, but then at last she came forward out of that rocky topography of the heart and pulled the little metal stool closer to the bed and reached for her and held her, annoyed only that her daughter made no motion of response, not to lean in or to grasp her mother's hand or do anything but weep and weep.

"It's for your own good," Evelyn said. "You don't want a baby now. Your whole life is in front of you."

"But I want to see him. That's all. Can't I just see him?"

"It's not a good idea."

"Why not?"

"Because it's just not. That's what they told me."

"Who?"

"The people at the orphanage."

"What did they say?" These words coming in short brief gasps between the sobbing.

"Just to make it as quick as possible."

"Did he look—what did he look like?"

Evelyn did not answer at first. The question seemed to rake across her like a sheet of sandpaper.

"Mama?"

She shook her head.

"Mama, what did he look like?"

"You know what he looked like."

"No I don't. I don't," she said. "I don't know because I didn't get to see him. I don't know anything. He's my baby. Mine!"

"He looked like a Jap, Helen," Evelyn said now. "Is that what you wanted to know? Does that help you get a picture?"

"Why are you saying that?"

"Because that's the truth."

"I love him."

"You don't know what love is," Evelyn said.

"Just get away. Just leave me alone and get away from me."

"Fine," Evelyn said. She stood and smoothed her blouse and went to the chair where she had draped the winter coat she had borrowed from her sister.

"It'll be all right, honey," Dottie said from her station across the room. "You'll see. It'll be just fine."

"No it won't," Helen said, her voice tortured with emotion. "It'll never be fine."

"Now you're just being dramatic," Evelyn said.

"Get out of here!" This came at a volume that was surprising even to Evelyn, who had heard every screech and wail of the girl's life, a kind of primal shriek that brought Evelyn upright in an instant, her hand flashing through the air, and the impact of her palm against her daughter's face bringing with it a loud sharp crack.

"You shut your mouth," Evelyn said. "You're being a baby. That's why I had to take care of it for you. Because you're not capable of doing it yourself."

Helen stared at her mother, eyes wide and brimming with tears, one hand held to her reddening cheek.

Dottie had come up behind Evelyn, her own hand soft on her older sister's shoulder. "Come on, Lynnie," she said. "It's time to go. Helen needs her rest."

"Not a word of thanks for what I've done," Evelyn said, her tone flat.

"Just leave me alone," this phrase repeated twice and then a third time as Dottie's hand pulled gently on her sister's shoulder and Evelyn at last allowed herself to be turned from the hospital bed. From behind them a nurse entered the

room, her bright voice announcing her presence even before
she appeared in the doorway, and Evelyn spun to that sound,
her mood changing all at once to match. "Why yes that *is*
good news."

Helen continued to snivel quietly from her attitude of recline
upon the heap of rubbery pillows, as fragile and insubstantial
as a bundle of twigs.

———

"BUT YOU HAVE TO UNDERSTAND," Mrs. Wilson was saying,
"that I thought I was doing what was best for my family. You
have to understand that."

"Mrs. Wilson."

"She was just a little girl. Seventeen years old. She didn't
know what she was doing, not really, and it was her whole future
out ahead of her."

"Mrs. Wilson."

"What would you have done had it been one of your own
daughters? What would you have—"

"Evelyn."

My eyes had been bouncing back and forth between them as
if I were watching a tennis match but now Mrs. Wilson stopped
speaking, the flow of words clipped off and the living room ringing with silence.

"I don't understand what you're telling me," Mrs.
Takahashi said.

"Why, I'm trying—I'm trying to tell you about the baby."
Her eyes flashed around the room, bright and wet.

"Helen's baby."

"Yes, Helen's, but also . . . oh God, Kim. Oh God how can I say it?"

I could see it in her eyes then, Mrs. Takahashi's, the dawning of understanding. First disbelief and then the whole of those years flooding out before her from those days of simple distrust in Newcastle to the night of the stillborn child to the buses on that May afternoon to this moment in her own living room twenty-seven years later, a life I did not even know or understand yet, but which would remain with me in the years to follow, the pieces sometimes coming unbidden and filling in the gaps and details until the whole of it seemed to rest upon my heart: the seeping slats of their barracks room in Tule Lake, the peaches and plums and pears, the long days she had spent in Oakland and finally San Jose, her daughters growing, marrying, her husband still working at the grocery where he had worked since the days just after the war, all of time shifting and moving and turning under her, and that one thing, that one event seeming to rush in across that great spinning disc all at once. She had not said his name in years and years, not out loud, instead keeping it like a soft warm sphere inside her body, intoning it when she chanted with the other practitioners at the church—Namu Amida Butsu Namu Amida Butsu—and which she sometimes heard ringing in her heart. Now it felt as if it had simply been rotating upon time's great disc all the while and now had come to swing in under her, the name rising through her feet and legs and belly and heart so that when it came to her voice at last it exhaled out of her in a long, quiet breath, its sound seeming to come independent of her throat but alive unto itself: "Raymond."

"Yes," Mrs. Wilson said.

"Raymond's child. With Helen?"

"Yes."

"And you—" She felt the room tightening now, its walls seeming to draw inward even as her breath caught in her throat, her own room, her own living room with its furniture, with its plastic fruit on the coffee table and the block print of Mount Fuji upon the wall. "You gave the baby away?"

"To the nuns at the Catholic orphanage. In Seattle. But that's why I came, Kim. That's why I came here. Because I need you." Evelyn's voice had risen now, not becoming emotional but simply becoming louder, clearer, like a bell ringing in the empty sky.

But when Kimiko spoke next, her own voice was almost silence itself. "Please leave my home," she said simply.

"Kim . . ."

"Get out of my home," Mrs. Takahashi said.

Mrs. Wilson said nothing now and for a long while neither she nor I moved, the room around us choking down until it felt as if all the oxygen had fled, leaving us with our mouths agape as if fish flung up from the sea. Then Mrs. Wilson came to her feet, her mouth closing and her lips forming a thin hard line, her entire body rigid. "I'm sorry," she whispered. And then, before I could even stand, she was out the door, the broad white shape of it closing hard behind her.

I set my delicate cup upon the coffee table and stood, still not quite knowing how to behave. "Thank you for the tea," I mumbled, nodding and then half bowing, embarrassed by that latter action but not knowing what else to do or how to excuse myself, but if Mrs. Takahashi noticed me at all she made no indication of it until I was at the door, my hand upon the knob.

"Boy or girl?" she said then.

"What do you mean?"

"Was the baby a boy or a girl?" She sat forward in the chair, her hands upon her lap, unmoving, not looking at me, not looking at anything.

"I don't know," I said simply. Then I opened the door and passed into the bright clear summer sunlight.

6

WE DID NOT SPEAK ON THE DRIVE BACK FROM SAN JOSE and I was left to wonder just what I had overheard, the story of that birth in Seattle, Mrs. Wilson and her sister, Dottie, and the baby and Mrs. Wilson's daughter, Helen. And Ray Takahashi of course, whose name I had not heard before that afternoon.

Something of the story stayed with me that night, after we had returned to my grandmother's home and Mrs. Wilson had driven away into the early evening, the sun low and the oaks casting long shadows across the golden summer grasses. My grandmother could hardly understand my questions, although she confirmed that Helen Wilson was, indeed, Evelyn Wilson's daughter.

"I didn't even know she had children," I told her.

"A daughter and a son," my grandmother told me. "Helen married someone from out of town. Maybe Chicago. Or Minneapolis? Sales, I think. Must have been twenty years ago now."

She was able to fill in some of the details of Mrs. Wilson's life, for my grandmother had never left Placer County and had the narrative advantage of that constant stream of old-timers passing through the living room nearly every day of the week, bringing with them a rich and colorful variety of local gossip. Perhaps it was for this reason that I did not tell my grandmother the specifics of what I had heard in Mrs. Takahashi's living room, offering instead a vague rendition comprised mostly of the small talk that had begun the visit, Mrs. Wilson's asking about the health and well-being of Mrs. Takahashi's husband and so on. Of course Mrs. Wilson herself had asked me not to speak of what I had heard, an admonition delivered as I pulled to a stop in front of my grandmother's house. She handed me thirty dollars in cash, more than twice what I made at the gas station during a full eight-hour shift and which I tried feebly to refuse.

"John," she said to me after that transaction was complete. Her eyes had met mine and for the first time that day her focus was fully turned toward me; I could feel her gaze like heat on my face. "I don't know what you think you heard and I can't really ask you to keep a secret for me, I mean you don't owe me anything, but I'd appreciate it very much if you'd . . . if you could, I mean . . ."

"Don't worry, Mrs. Wilson," I said. "I don't know who I'd tell anyway."

She seemed to glance behind me toward the house in which my grandmother was, even now, peeking through the screen.

"I won't say a word," I said.

She nodded, her mouth once again a tight line.

In a way, my silence was a strange thing to agree to, for as Mrs. Wilson herself had pointed out, I had no reason to feel any particular loyalty to her at all, apart, I suppose, from the notion of our being related in some distant fashion. And yet I knew I would not tell my grandmother what I had heard in Mrs. Takahashi's living room, knew it even before Mrs. Wilson asked for my silence. I cannot explain why except to say that it felt private to me, perhaps almost holy, and that even holding this information in trust marked me as a member of what I already assumed was a tiny circle: myself and Mrs. Wilson and Helen, if she was even still alive, and Mrs. Wilson's sister and now Mrs. Takahashi. It was clear even from listening in utter silence that no one else knew at all.

And of course I understood why Mrs. Wilson had taken her daughter north to Seattle, why she had removed her daughter's changing shape from the prying eyes of gossiping neighbors, just as I understood why it was that she did not want me to mention a word of it to my grandmother. Who knows what excuse she gave at the time? Perhaps she simply said she was off to visit her sister. And would anyone have paid a scrap of attention to such a claim? It was a time not unlike that in which I sat later with Chiggers on my grandmother's back porch, when the names of local boys appeared in the newspaper with regularity, and with them a slowly twisting feeling that death had come with his scythe to waltz among the oaks.

And so why would anyone have paid the slightest attention to Helen Wilson and her mother traveling north to Seattle or even staying there for eight or ten months? In 1943 the county felt as if it had been drained down to its bare skeleton: the Japanese gone, the boys gone, and with them both of the Wilson children, Jimmy off to the army (I would learn this soon enough), and Helen to the great Pacific Northwest. And to think that Ray

Takahashi did not know that he had, while interned at Tule Lake, become a father at the age of twenty, just days before he had been allowed at long last to sign up for the army himself, that he had a child who was, even in that moment, being looked after by the Sisters of Mercy in that rain-soaked forestland at the edge of the cold, churning Pacific.

Of course I did not even know that much at the time. The rest would begin to come after Mrs. Wilson appeared at the filling station a second time, pulling up to the pump much as she had weeks earlier. By then I had finished reading Styron's book about Nat Turner and had returned, in the interim, to *Look Homeward, Angel*, a book which I had already read twice before, once in Vietnam, its sentences consuming me. *O lost, and by the wind grieved, ghost, come back again.*

I had heard the car but had not yet seen it as I left the hot shadows of the office and stepped into the bright heat of the direct sun. Then the Pontiac and there, framed in the window, the face of my aunt, her eyes already trained on mine.

"Mrs. Wilson," I said.

"Good morning, John," she replied, not smiling—she never really seemed to smile—but at least nodding in a way that I thought was intended to be amiable, her stark angular features once again framed by a gauzy scarf that fanned out over the rounded mass of her hair.

She waited until I had filled the car and washed the windows and retrieved her change from the office before asking me what she had plainly come there to ask, the Pontiac requiring little more than a top-off. Of course I said yes. Even without the pay I was strangely intrigued by the shades of narrative I had been witness to during the previous visit. And there was another reason as well. On my days off I had taken to sitting in front of my typewriter and drinking—beer at first and eventually sipping from a bottle of vodka I kept hidden under my bed. In my writerly naïveté, I thought, at the time, that the drinking was but a shadow of my inability to get my writing done, my attempt to lubricate my imagination quickened by each hour in which the page was yet empty. It did not occur me, and would not for many years, that much of that impediment was held within the greasy confines of the bottle itself. Simply put, I needed something with which to occupy my thoughts and my imagination. Something besides Vietnam. And so it was that midweek, on my day off from the station, my aunt once again met me at my grandmother's home and we set off once more for San Jose.

———

MRS. TAKAHASHI ALMOST SEEMED to be expecting us this time. Again she stood on the little porch of her bungalow when we pulled to a stop, watching as we exited the car and, also like the first time, Mrs. Wilson was pulled up short by that unwavering gaze. Both of them remained silent until we had reached the base of the little run of steps that led up to the porch and entrance, at which point Mrs. Takahashi said a single word: "Tea?" And when Mrs. Wilson did not answer, I did: "Please," and Mrs. Takahashi turned and entered the house, leaving the door open behind her.

She was in the kitchen for some time, during which Mrs. Wilson and I sat in utter and total silence. When Mrs. Takahashi appeared at last it was with the same tray she had brought during our previous visit: the three cups—two ornate and delicate and one heavy and thick—the creamer, the little bowl of sugar cubes. "How are you, John?" she said quietly.

"Me?" I said. "I'm all right. I'm fine."

"It's kind of you to do the driving," she said.

"It's not a problem," I mumbled.

My aunt was silent all this time and had been mostly so from the moment we had driven away from Newcastle, but now, at the sound of Mrs. Takahashi's voice, she began to stir, opening her purse and removing a single small sheet of paper. She glanced up now but when Mrs. Takahashi did not step forward to retrieve the sheet she lay it faceup on the table and then returned to her rigid posture, seated at the front end of the sofa's pad so that she seemed ready, at any moment, to flee.

She looked down briefly at the sheet. "That's all I know," she said quietly.

I could not see what the paper contained from where I sat and Mrs. Takahashi did not so much as glance at it on the table, keeping her eyes focused on the woman who sat stiff and upright upon her sagging sofa. Mrs. Takahashi continued to stand near the arched doorway that led into the kitchen.

I wondered at first if the two women would return to the strange idleness and prolonged silences that had marked my first visit to this living room, but then Mrs. Takahashi's voice came, forceful despite its calm, thin sound: "You kept this from us for twenty-seven years," she said.

"Yes," Mrs. Wilson said simply. "You have every right to be angry with me."

"Why did you come now? Why didn't you just leave it quiet? We would never have known."

"Because I wanted Raymond's help."

"Raymond's help?"

"To find the child. I thought maybe the courts would open the record if Raymond asked them to. As the father, I mean."

"Raymond?" Mrs. Takahashi's voice, Kimiko's, sounded distant and alone, as if in a different room.

"Yes," Mrs. Wilson said. "That's what I thought. And if he doesn't want to help me, I can understand that. After what I did. Keeping it from him."

"Raymond's gone," Kimiko said.

"Gone where?"

"He never came back from the war." For a long moment Kimiko stood unmoving. No one spoke. I looked from her to my aunt and back again. Finally Kimiko mumbled, "Maybe something to eat," and turned and stepped out of the room.

"Kim? Kim?" Evelyn said behind her, her voice rising in volume, on her feet now, following Mrs. Takahashi into the kitchen and me following dumbly behind them both as if I might offer some assistance. Mrs. Takahashi bustled around the small room, opening a cabinet and removing a tin of cookies and then retrieving a plate. "What do you mean, he never came back from the war?" Mrs. Wilson said.

Mrs. Takahashi looked at her now but said nothing, and after a moment she returned to the tin and opened it and began laying cookies upon the plate in the shape of a circle.

"My God," my aunt said then. "I don't understand it."

"You don't understand what?"

"I don't understand where he might have gone."

"He didn't go anywhere," Mrs. Takahashi said, turning to face her now.

"No, no," my aunt said. She had stepped forward and now

stood in the center of the room, her breath coming fast. "You mean you never saw him?"

Mrs. Takahashi said nothing, only stared in silence.

"He came back," my aunt said. "He did come back, Kim. He was in town. In Newcastle. In his uniform." And, after a moment: "Maybe you should sit down. We don't need anything to eat. Kim? Kim? Are you all right?"

For a moment the woman looked as if she had turned completely to stone, even her flesh seeming to tilt gray, and when she sat at last, in a curved vinyl-padded chair that she jerked from beneath a small table, she did so as an act of crumbling decay. My aunt's presence must have felt a kind of tidal wave set to wipe clean everything she had built for herself in San Jose, only a few hours from Newcastle and yet a world away, a world better and more secure and more like home than any she had experienced before the war.

At long last Mrs. Takahashi's voice came from her seat at the little table: a dry sound, like paper rubbing against sand, a sound as unfriendly and pained as any I have ever heard in my life. "Tell me what you know of my boy," she said.

Like her narrative of the birth of her daughter's child, Mrs. Wilson's account of Raymond Takahashi's return to Placer County was faltering and confused. Only later, just before the summer faded into the chill of fall, would I learn just how incomplete her account was, the narrative she spun disjointed because she was, at every step, erasing herself and her family from its shape. In Mrs. Takahashi's kitchen we were (Mrs. Takahashi and I) offered a tale told out of order, so that it seemed at first that Raymond returned and immediately departed again. Mrs. Takahashi finally had to stop her and

ask, "How long?" and even then Mrs. Wilson seemed to dis-
semble, her bearing rigid even as her head jerked and twitched
like that of a distressed bird. "Well, I don't know exactly. He
was there and then one day he was just gone. I don't know
when he left."

"But how long do you think he was there?"

"I don't really know—"

"Mrs. Wilson—"

"It might have been a month. Six weeks maybe."

"Six weeks?" Mrs. Takahashi said now, her amazement plain
in her voice. "He was in Newcastle for six weeks?"

"Well, like I said, it's difficult to say."

So her son had returned home from the war, had survived it,
but somehow in all that time had failed to contact his parents
at all, had not sent a telegram, had not written a postcard, had
instead lived in and around Newcastle for as long as forty-two
days, forty-two days in which he had been alive and she had not
even known it, a time during which he had been no farther than
my aunt and I had driven that very day, a matter of hours, a
span of time so slight that even to consider that her son had been
that close and alive and she had not even known it felt to her like
a direct repudiation of everything she had already reconciled
herself to believe: that her beloved son had been killed fighting
for the same country that had put not only himself but also his
mother and father and his two sisters behind barbed wire. But
that had not been the case.

"It's not possible," Mrs. Takahashi said now. "We searched
everywhere. My husband even went back to Newcastle to look.
He wasn't there."

"I didn't know that," Mrs. Wilson said.

"You're mistaken. It was someone else you saw."

"I'm not mistaken, Kim. I don't know why you didn't find him. Maybe your husband came before your son got to California, or after he left. Raymond was there. I swear he was."

"Tell me what happened," she said, her voice a dry rasp. They were both sitting now, Mrs. Takahashi on one side of the little table, Mrs. Wilson on the other, the two woman flanking the window through which bright yellow light glowed without direction or angle.

"I am," Mrs. Wilson said. "I have."

"From the beginning."

Mrs. Wilson's body seemed, for the briefest moment, to slump, to drain, before righting itself again, the spine once more in a long ruler-straight line from waist to head. "It was a long time ago," she said now, and when Mrs. Takahashi began to speak again she lifted a hand and the other woman fell immediately to silence. "But I'll try," Mrs. Wilson said.

When she began again, Mrs. Wilson indeed started at the beginning, although it was not quite the opening scene I have supplied here. In her retelling, she was told that Ray had returned by her orchard foreman and had only seen him from a distance—perhaps in town or in Auburn a few times—so that there was, in effect, very little to tell.

"You have to remember everything," Mrs. Takahashi said.

"But I'm sorry I just don't."

"Who else did he talk to?"

"I don't know, Kim."

"Where did he stay?"

"I'm not sure." She paused then. "Maybe at the church? I know some of the Japs—I'm sorry—the Japanese stayed there. At least that's what I heard."

"The Methodists?"

"No, I meant the Buddhist church. But yes maybe the Methodists too."

Mrs. Takahashi looked at her for a long moment, the expression on her face one of absolute wonder. "So they knew?" she said after a time.

"Who did?" This came from me, my question exploding out without warning so that both women turned immediately to look as if they had forgotten I still remained in the room.

"The Japanese," she said.

"We just thought he went back to live with you," Mrs. Wilson said then. "You know. He was there for a while and then we just didn't see him anymore."

She shook her head. "He never came to us. I don't understand why he would go there at all."

Mrs. Wilson did not respond. It was all too much. She had come to Mrs. Takahashi to enlist her help only to be faced with something else entirely, the realization that Raymond Takahashi's mother had believed, all these years, that her son had perished in the war even though the army had informed her (her husband really, for it had been he who had written the Secretary of the Army) that he had been discharged. They had entered a period of panic then—this I would learn later—calling the Buddhist church, calling those few orchardists who had returned to Placer County, only to be told again and again that Raymond had not been seen, Hiro even driving there to speak to the priest in person and to be told this same information yet again. I believe now that Hiro missed finding news of his son by mere days, for his visit to Placer County must have been only a week or two before Raymond's arrival, so that when Raymond himself had visited the church and the priest there had told him that his father had come looking for him, Raymond's response must have been to thank the priest and to tell him a lie: that he had already returned to visit his parents and sisters and that there was no need to worry. He was a dutiful son. The priest would have nodded and smiled and that would have been the end of it. There would have been no reason for the priest or anyone else to contact the Takahashis in Oakland. Meanwhile, his parents continued to write the army, once, twice, a dozen times, asking for explanation and finally coming to accept the only truth that seemed possible: that Raymond was dead, that he had perished in Italy or Germany or France and that the army, through what her husband had called a "clerical error," had neglected to report it correctly. But now this, this new knowledge, which Mrs. Wilson was beginning to understand, and I with her, was yet more important than any secret pregnancy or even of the existence of the child.

Still Mrs. Wilson did not tell her of Raymond's appearance on her porch that hot summer day, or of what she learned later about his altercation with her foreman, Bob Campo, nor did she offer any real specificity of what she knew of his movements in the county, despite the fact that she had followed those movements with some care. Her only goal at that time had been to keep him away from Helen at all costs, but her daughter was almost twenty then and had been dating a local boy, a white boy, and it was therefore nearly impossible to keep her indoors.

"I'm sorry, Kim," Mrs. Wilson said. "I just assumed he'd gone to find you."

For a long while the room rang with silence.

"I don't understand it," Mrs. Takahashi said at last. "I just don't understand it at all."

7

"so wait—where was he, then?"

"Who?"

"Jesus, Flip, who do you think? The Jap kid."

This was but a few days after I had returned from San Jose. The man I sat with I knew wholly by the nickname he had borne in Vietnam. I have no real notion of how it was in other units, but in ours most of us had nicknames of some kind, some colorful, some mere abbreviations of the names our parents might have called us, so that amidst Phil and Skip and Mike there was also Apache Dan and Mark-One and Tenn (short for Tennessee) and the great gruff African-American philosopher we all called Mama and the thin reedy stoner poet known to us as Professor Ted. And there was the man who sat across from me in the booth: my friend Chiggers, a man with whom I had lived and died in the mangrove swamps and whom I loved in the way that men who have been in combat together loved each other, many of our number bleeding out into the muck or exploded into pieces unrecognizable as human flesh. Those of us who survived had promised each other that we would stay in touch and that we would visit one another and be there for weddings and christenings and the like, and perhaps in the moment of our parting some of us actually believed such things were possible. But the truth was that I did not really think I would ever see any of them again after leaving the delta, not even Chiggers, who had been my best friend there. Indeed it had come to feel, in the year or so I had been stateside, that the war had been some strange dream from which I had never entirely awakened. It had all happened *over there*, in that other place, in another world than this. That the war was still ongoing did not seem possible, and yet it was present on a daily basis in the papers and on television and it would not be stilled.

And so it was strange to see Chiggers now. He had called my parents' home in Alhambra and they in turn had given him my grandmother's number. His voice through those miles of electric cable had sounded not unlike the crackling sound of my radio, and for a moment, so fleeting it was hardly present at all, I felt myself back in the muck and mud and blood, back in the fear, but then that sensation was gone and I was on the phone in my grandmother's living room, listening to Chiggers tell me that he would be on the way to Oregon to attend his cousin's wedding and could he stop by. I said yes and gave him my grandmother's address. When he finally arrived we drove around some and got more than half stoned on the fine Southern California pot he had brought with him from San Diego. Now we occupied a booth at a mostly deserted Denny's restaurant attached to a long rambling motel pressed hard against the interstate at the very edge of Auburn, the seat of Placer County and a town of six thousand or so souls.

I had never seen Chiggers outside of the military, and the man before me did not much resemble the man I had known in Vietnam. He had exchanged his fatigues and buzz cut for a denim shirt, pointed beard, and shaggy hair, not quite what we would have called long in 1969 but certainly on its way. It is a strange thing to say but in Vietnam I had never thought of him as Hispanic. Though he sometimes joked about being Mexican and peppered his curses with Spanish, what we did in Vietnam and who we were in that country seemed to diminish those differences, or rather made them irrelevant, although for me to say such a thing as a white man is problematic in ways I have tried to untangle for all the years since. Sitting across from me in that booth at Denny's in that small town, Chiggers looked like the scruffy Latino mechanic he had been before the war, a life he had returned to afterwards, and I, for all my friendship and love, wondered what the other patrons in the restaurant thought of us, both of us bunny-eyed and giggling like crazy people.

How strange that hardly a year before we stood together in the Forest of Assassins, the radio's antenna waving in the air like a great black arrow pointing ever and always to my blood and bone. The fact that we both escaped the entirety of the war unmarred in body if not in spirit did not speak of skill or even of luck but instead only of randomness. Chiggers, being Catholic, might well have felt otherwise, but I could not understand how one could hold fast to the idea of a benevolent God watching over one's physical and moral self in the midst of what was, quite literally, a quagmire. And now we sat smoking and drinking endless coffee in the landscape of my childhood. What world was this? How did this world and the Forest of Assassins exist simultaneously? Along a muddy canal, a line of thatch-roofed hootches exploded into gouts of bright orange flame. How many human beings had been inside? A half dozen? A dozen? More? Men and women and children burned alive. We counted them all as VC kills. And in all the ways I could tabulate, every one of those kills had been mine. Hot contact north river. Yankee Sierra. Zero-One. Five-Seven. Six-Two. Smoking purple haze. And then straining to hear the impossible shriek of the Phantoms as they came screaming down their fire from on high.

Chiggers and I had already talked about some of the guys from the old company but neither of us had any real information to share. One of our squad members was getting married—we had both received wedding invitations—but he lived in rural Alabama and that provided excuse enough not to attend. We mumbled about money but in fact we simply did not want to see him acting as if life were normal and that it would go on despite all we had done and all we had failed to do.

I do not know why I began to tell him of the first time I drove Mrs. Wilson to San Jose. Perhaps it was only because that trip had begun something which had managed to hold my own interest sufficiently enough for me to expend some effort in investigating its contours. I had begun telling him of the strange conversation in Mrs. Takahashi's living room and then swerved into a long digression that ended with the buses departing the square. That Chiggers, stoned as he was, could somehow remember where the story had begun was a kind of miracle. He had asked what had happened to Ray Takahashi and now sat as expectant as a Labrador, smiling and awaiting my response.

"I don't know what happened to him," I told him. "Nobody knows."

"But his girl had a baby."

"Yeah that's right."

"His baby."

I nodded.

"So he came back to find her?"

"He might have," I said, "but really I don't think he knew."

"About the baby?" Chiggers sucked at his cigarette. "Why'd he come back, then?"

"Nobody knows that either."

"Ay, Dios mío," Chiggers said then. "Nobody knows nothing about nothing."

"I guess not," I said, realizing as I said it that it was not, in fact, much of a story to tell, and we fell back to sipping at our coffees and puffing at our cigarettes. I wondered how much more pot he had in the paper bag in his car and how much money I could scrape together to buy some before he was once again on the road to Oregon.

Chiggers might have looked different in some ways but he had not changed; he was still and ever would be the same old Chiggers from Dong Tam and the Plain of Reeds and the million nameless waterways that snaked endlessly through the mangroves and palms and cocoa trees, those shadowed tunnels that seem, even now, to pull me toward whatever horrors lay curtained by their green light.

The waitress brought our meals then. Chiggers's plate was

piled high with eggs and sausage and bacon and pancakes like a monument to all the breakfasts we wished for in Vietnam. Mine was much the same.

———

CHIGGERS TOLD ME upon arrival that he would need to be back on the road as soon as possible and yet our evening at Denny's wore on, and at some point he suggested that he might wander over to the motel desk to see what a room might cost him. It was then that I suggested my grandmother's sofa, small though it was. "The old lady won't mind?" Chiggers said, smiling his familiar grin.

"I'll need to ask her," I said, "but I think she'll be fine with it."

And she was, not only fine with it but seemingly relieved, as if his presence provided a temporary salve for some aspect of my life that she had questioned. She asked if we needed something to eat or drink and then retired to her bedroom. We moved to the porch off the back of the house then, its nightscape a small box of overgrown grass—I should have cut it but had not—and a gnarled old plum tree laden with fruit, the rotten scent of which sometimes wafted across to us in the dark and infrequent breeze. It may have been a poor choice to sit in the dark like that—we might have retired, instead, to the boozy back room of that Denny's with its dingy bar and dance floor—for Chiggers's presence had brought a quickness to my chest, a feeling that the great span of the Pacific had folded over on itself in the night so that the seventy-eight hundred miles that separated me from the Nine Dragon River had lessened and lessened until I could almost—but not quite—see the tracer rounds red-lining across the black sky beyond the fence.

"I'm glad you're okay, man," Chiggers said.

"Yeah, well, I'm glad you're okay too," I told him.

He was silent for a long time, puffing at his cigarette. In the night all around us, there yet remained a sense of sun-heat radiating up through the deck boards, from the trees, from the grass, but the air itself had cooled enough that I felt gooseflesh rise to my skin. From the dark shadows of the yard's shaggy verdancy came the overlapping chirp of crickets beyond which drifted the occasional shush of cars on the interstate or the great choking moan of a diesel truck barreling downhill against its gearbox. I tried to find words that might divert Chiggers from the drift of his own mind but nothing would come and at last his voice reappeared from the shadows. "It's just that, well, you know, you kinda faded out toward the end there," he said. "I mean we all did, right, but after Phil and Dan and all that shit. That was a hard time."

"It was all a hard time."

"You know what I mean." Chiggers pulled on his cigarette. Mine had been smoked down to the nub. For reasons I could hardly articulate, I suddenly and inexplicably wanted him to leave. I had tried not to think of him or any of them. Although I never moved much further than the one piece in *Esquire* and the various note cards stacked by the typewriter in my grandmother's spare bedroom, when I thought of Vietnam it was almost always as a source of fiction. The quality of invention offered a tangible albeit illusory sense of control that extended not just to the landscape but to specific situations and characters, so that even though my fictional squadmates lived and died in ways not so far removed from their actual counterparts, the role of random and unfeeling overlord was not that of some distant God but was rather my own. I could ponder the feeling of it all and the topography and the intensity of the green, and the unmitigated liquid seep, and the high metallic shriek of gunfire, and the bright eruptions of orange flame when the Phantoms came low and obliterated their targets, but the actual facts of my own experience I held in secret, a feat of memory which I recommitted to each night. So I had tried not to think of any of them. Not Phil or Apache Dan or Skip or Mark-One or Mama or Professor Ted. Not even Chiggers.

My fear in that moment was that Chiggers would want to talk through it all. I expected his voice to come out of the darkness, from the point of his cigarette: "Do you remember what Professor Ted said that time when we were in the boat on the Vàm Cỏ Đông?" and I would say, "You mean the time when we called in the air strike on that village?" and he would say, "Which village? There were a million fucking villages," and I would say, "Two million," and he would say something like, "Three," and then, "You loved your radio, ese. Call in the big guns," and I would say, "No doubt about that," and we would both laugh. I had called in so many air strikes that neither of us could have ever kept count of them all, and we would go on like that, maybe all night.

But he did not say this or anything like it. Perhaps Chiggers too felt the need to both talk and not talk about that time in our lives. Perhaps acknowledging that we were both okay was enough because it acknowledged that although we were alive neither of us was really okay or ever would be.

———

CHIGGERS TOOK THE FLOOR of my room, as I knew my grand-mother would be up and about early in the morning and I knew too that my friend and I would sleep well past her waking. I could hear him begin snoring almost immediately. That simple sound might have gotten us all killed just a year earlier, a thought which reminded me that in many ways I had never really left that place. I had mustered out in April and yet there remained a sense of humidity in the dark thick muscle of my heart, that tight fist continuing to pump even as all those others—friends and companions and enemies too—had disappeared into the flat relaxed palm of death. In the end, they loaded me into a 747 filled with similar survivors, only a few of whom I knew at all, Chiggers among them, and that great silver ship had lifted into the sky and we, those who had lived through it, burst, as one, into applause. The landscape that shrank beneath the windows of the plane had become synonymous with death, from the suck-ing mud to the biting ants and snakes to the water buffalo and grass-roofed villages standing in the deep green of palms and reeds, the very richness, the living fecundity of the place predi-cated upon the simultaneity of its rank and fetid decay. And yet from the air it looked a tropical paradise, prelapsarian in its beauty and grace, its shape shining through the vaporous scrim of my own escape, my own understanding that I was alive, that I was still alive.

Nestled in my duffel on that flight were the notebooks and cards that now sat next to the disused typewriter under the win-dow just a few feet from where I lay. I did not need to thumb through that material to recall what it contained: a series of disjointed and garbled ideas, sentences, fragments, character names without explanation, dates without referent, untethered and unexplained anecdotes ("tell them about the goose" and "bbq at the Bon Mot" and "Chesty's dream"). It occurs to me now that there is likely a wealth of possible fictions to be found in those notes, but at the time they felt a kind of flood that washed over my imagination with such force that I could hardly stand to look at them, leaving my brain simply empty of ideas, empty even of sentences.

The members of my company were good men on the whole but Chiggers was the one to whom I felt the closest. I wanted to talk endlessly about books and writers and he seemed perfectly willing to listen and even to comment and ask questions and challenge what I took as basic and inviolable facts. I believed Faulkner was a better writer than Hemingway and that Thomas Wolfe was the best of them all. I liked Saul Bellow and Norman Mailer and James Jones. Chiggers had come from a world I had sometimes glimpsed when I had lived in Southern California and the stories he told of his extended Catholic family, both in Mexico and scattered up and down the West Coast from San Diego to Seattle, were filled with hilarity and heartbreak. He had lived through travails the likes of which I could only dream about and had come through them tough and open and honest and loyal. I envied that about him, that he had such experiences to draw power from, and I wished I had something similar in my own life but my experiences, up to that point, felt unilaterally shallow and pointless.

The base at which we were then stationed consisted of a great sea of tents and cinder-block buildings and plywood structures set in series of staggered and ill-fitting gridworks upon a field of endless mud surrounded by rice paddies and thick jungle. Along the southern boundary ran the brown flow of one of the innumerable rivers that comprised the delta. There was a small Vietnamese town nearby, a town constructed during the French occupation of the region and one therefore rumored to be quite beautiful in the manner of quaint and tender imperialism, but we regular grunts were not allowed to go there and in all the time I was stationed at that muddy base I never once walked its French-inflected streets.

We were, indeed, near-prisoners of the base, which made my feeling of isolation all the more acute. It was into this deep well of loneliness that I poured myself, my obsession with words and writers and writing reaching a kind of fever pitch in the first months of my time in that mud field, an obsession broken only momentarily by the mixture of boredom and terror that struck me each time my unit was ordered outside the wire and into the jungle beyond. I had learned very early that were I to die in Vietnam, my death was unlikely to be in actual combat but rather via a form of random deliverance impossible to predict or to fight against: a sniper's bullet, a land mine, or any number of nefarious and ingenious booby traps set by the invisible enemy. I had read Norman Mailer's *The Naked and the Dead* and had imagined war with a clear enemy who would be fierce and uniformed and would be, of course, indisputably in the wrong, and we would fight them on terms agreed upon by both sides using the military might we had each built and the training we had each received. But in fact it was wholly unclear what we were trying to do in those endless islands and waterways, the whole of it seeming to rise up from beneath us like the incoming tides, leaving only the great twisted vertical shapes of the mangroves towering from that muddy influx.

Two months shy of my return from that country, my unit took fire from a thick dark tangle of jungle near the village of Cái Bè. We had been out beyond the wire for several days and I had the increasingly claustrophobic feeling that sometimes came upon me when I felt certain that death's bony fingers were preparing to pull me under the malarial waters, so when the first shots rang out I was almost relieved, for the waiting, at least, was over. I could hear Chiggers shouting from somewhere to my left and the others scattering everywhere through the shallow mire. And already my friends were dying. Phil. Apache Dan. Professor Ted.

I did not know I had been screaming until I dialed air command and had to stop long enough to relay a set of coordinates. There was no order given me and the coordinates I shouted into the handset would bring half the jungle to our north to flame. When I was done I lay down in the mud, my hands on my helmet, listening to the rounds zip into the brown water and tick through the trees and foliage all around. I could hear, as if from very far away, the sounds of the others in my unit—those still alive—their voices raised against the onslaught of their own firepower.

I was a coward. I did not return fire. Not that day. Instead I lay on my back in the crushed grass, staring up at the sky and weeping and waiting for the F-4s. When that great screeching came at last I rolled to my belly to watch as the trees went black and the whole world beyond burst into a wall of orange flame. I had seen countless air strikes but this had been the most magnificent and I shouted at the sight of those acres and acres gone bright with fire.

When they took the dead away and Chiggers and I and the others wandered through the char of that long swath of destruction, what we found beyond was a burned and desolate village of the dead, among its razed reed structures a cinder-block building, likely built by the U.S. Army as a show of goodwill, its walls still intact but its roof fully burned away. The children within were tiny bone-black sculptures melted to their desks. And I ask you this: Are they more human to you because they are children?

"Fuck fuck fuck," our unit commander shouted. "Everyone out. We're getting the fuck out of here right now." And then, to me: "This is on you, you stupid fuck."

I do not think any of us in that unit ever really recovered from that day. Six of us were killed and the remainder who survived stumbled through the last two months of our sentence with a kind of grim and quiet determination. We did not talk of it. Had it not been for Chiggers I do not think I would have made it through, for he, at least, seemed capable of continuing to live with some semblance of grace and dignity and even humor. And it was Chiggers too who would, in the dark of the night when I could not stop weeping, tell me that he was grateful for what I had done. "You saved us," he would say. "Don't think of it any other way. You saved us."

Men, women, children, and water buffalo: all were counted among the enemy dead. Command pointed us in the supposed direction of the supposed enemy and so it was into that direction we poured the full liquid metal of our arsenal, the great hot barrage of it like a tunnel of teeth chewing the whole of the landscape down to stubble. God help anyone who stumbled into its path. I thought that if I could only articulate its voracity, on the page, that I might straighten my thoughts, my heart like a burnished disc of hot brass spinning endlessly in the tropic sunlight, its sound a continuous, susurrate hiss.

In the room, in the darkness, from the floor, Chiggers mumbled in his sleep. What I thought of was squelch and volume and my voice screaming into the handset. Whiskey Dragon to Rosebud. Hot contact. Hot contact. God I would do it all again if it meant I would live.

8

CHIGGERS LEFT FOR OREGON IN THE MORNING, PROMISING
me that he would stop by again on Wednesday or Thursday of
the following week, when his return to San Diego would bring
him back down the interstate. Had it turned out that way, some
of this story might have been different, but of course the stories
we tell about our lives, the true stories, can only describe what
actually occurred. We can act as if we might have chosen some
alternate path, all the while knowing that, had any of us the
ability to roll back time, we would, given the same information,
make the same cowardly decisions all over again. And all the
people I had a hand in killing would still be dead. And I would
still be alive.

"You take care, man," Chiggers said to me as I stood next
to his Fairlane, the vehicle so covered in road grime that it was
impossible to discern what color might lie beneath, the windshield fogged with grease and dirt and smeared insects.

"You too," I told him.

We shook hands briefly and then went into a one-armed embrace, our hands still clasped, Chiggers clapping me on the back once, then twice, and then holding me there, not quite embracing now but close enough that his mouth was at my ear. "You still think about it sometimes, right?" he said.

"Sure," I said. "Sure I do."

"I still hear them sometimes." His voice was barely a whisper. "Comin' out of the dark. And I can't tell if they're gooks or our guys. You know? I sometimes wake up screaming like I'm still there. Scares the shit out of my mom."

"I know," I said.

"I still feel like they're trying to kill me," he said.

"Me too."

He seemed to relax at that admission, and after a moment he released me from his embrace, his body sagging toward the car, be it in relief or exhaustion I did not know.

There was a different texture to talking about such things in the bright warm light of the morning, different than it had been even brushing up against those subjects in the darkness of my grandmother's back porch as the night rode on and on and our pot-stoked mellow flooded toward simple fatigue and finally to sleep. In a way, I was relieved that Chiggers was leaving, for I had sensed he wanted, more than anything, to talk about what had happened over there. But I was afraid that talking about it would bring the sluggish constant flow of the Nine Dragon River into a torrent, one which we would not be able to control or navigate and which would pull us both under its powerful current. How I wish now that I had held him there, had asked him to tell me more about how he felt, about how he was, but I did not. Sometimes I imagine myself telling him that he should picture me beside him when those black ghosts faded out of the shadows of that dream jungle, my radio warm and the handset of the Prick 10 already at my ear, already calling down a hellfire of salvation from the bright wet sky. But of course I said none of those things and Chiggers slipped behind the seat of the grime-encrusted Fairlane in silence, not speaking again until I had moved to walk back up the steps to my grandmother's. He called out my name then and I turned. Chiggers sat framed in the open window, his hair in dark greased furrows and his eyes black but his mouth upturned in a grin. "Got a present for you," he said. And when I reached the door he handed me, through the window, a paper sack. I could smell the pot within, its sticky aroma emanating everywhere. "Shit," I said, "let me get my wallet."

"It's a present," he said. "You can't pay for no present." Then the Fairlane roared to life, its engine rumbling low and heavy in my chest. And a few moments later he was gone.

———

"YOU LOOK TERRIBLE."

This a few days after Chiggers's departure as I stood in my grandmother's kitchen, wanting a cigarette or a cup of coffee or both, wanting something to do with my hands to keep them from shaking, having been drunk for much of the two days before, including, to a somewhat lesser extent, those hours I spent behind the counter at the filling station. I knew I was slipping toward some further darkness, and I knew that the drinking was only a half measure against it. Chiggers's visit had something to do with this spiral, although it was difficult to pinpoint exactly what his presence had done to me. Perhaps his departing admission that he still felt like someone was trying to kill him was enough to send me over the edge, if this was indeed what going over the edge felt like. All I really knew was that the measure the alcohol provided was insubstantial given the enormity of the great glass well into which all my fears seemed to swirl without end.

My grandmother, that morning, looked at me gravely, waiting for a response of some kind. She was not so directly critical of my behavior as my parents often were, especially her daughter, my mother, but there was perhaps a knot of criticism stuffed hard against her sense of concern, her eyes bright and watchful in the soft dry thin-lined whiteness of her face.

"I'm okay, Gran," I told her.

"You most certainly are not," she said. "I can smell the liquor on you from here."

"I've gotta get to work."

"You can't do that," she said now. "Not yet."

She rose and pulled me into the small confines of the washroom, one hand tight on my wrist, the other stoppering the claw-foot tub and turning the spigot on full.

"Hot bath," she said. "Cure all." Then she paused and said, "Well, not cure *all* but it'll help."

"I don't want to take a bath, Gran."

"And yet that's what you're gonna do."

"I'm not a child."

"Aren't you? I'll bring you a clean set of clothes and I'll set a cup of coffee right here on the counter. You can drink it in the tub if you want."

Then she left the room, the door swinging closed behind her. And because she was my grandmother and because I think I needed, more than anything else, for someone to simply tell me what it was I should do, I climbed into the blazing heat of the tub, sinking down to my chin and then submerging myself altogether, the ceiling above me wobbling in the rippling heat.

———

KIMIKO TAKAHASHI ARRIVED at the filling station a few days later. The feeling of terror that possessed me had dissipated but was not gone altogether. It would take a lifetime for that feeling to fade, if it ever did, if it ever has. At the very least I had managed to stop drinking in the daytime and was willing to count that as some small success.

I had heard the sedan stop at the pumps, the vehicle unfamiliar, its hood facing away from me so that I could only see the halo of dark hair around the driver's head. But once at the window I found myself staring down into Mrs. Takahashi's upturned face.

For a moment neither of us spoke, our simultaneous surprise rendering us both utterly speechless. Then I said quietly, "Oh," and then, "Mrs. Takahashi."

"John," she said. She looked through me for a moment, toward the office, and then looked back at me once more. "You work here?"

"That's right," I told her. "You're . . . are you . . . you're traveling through or . . ."

"I'm coming to see Mrs. Wilson," she said grimly, looking forward through the dirty windshield now.

"Right, of course," I said, and, as she made no further comment, I began to go about my general duties, cleaning the bug-spattered glass and filling the engine, and when I returned to the driver's side Mrs. Takahashi looked up at me, her eyes tinged, I thought, with emotion. "John, I wondered if you would do me a great favor," she said, her voice steady despite her bright, wet eyes.

I handed her the change and told her I would be happy to do whatever it was she needed. Mrs. Takahashi asked if I knew a place where she and Mrs. Wilson could meet, and when I asked her if she needed help getting to the Wilsons' her expression seemed to crumble in on itself like a pile of slightly damp sand. "I can't go up there," she said, her sentences ever tinged with the faint curl of her accent. "I thought I could but I can't." She looked up at me then. "You must think me very silly," she said, "driving all the way here from San Jose. An old lady. And now I can't even go up to a house and knock on a door."

I supposed I might have suggested the very Denny's restaurant where I had sat with Chiggers a few days before, or, for that matter, any of the other little cafés in town, but when I opened my mouth again what came was not the suggestion of a restaurant but of my grandmother's home. "It'll be private," I told her. "My grandmother won't bother us at all. You, I mean. And Mrs. Wilson."

First my old war buddy and now Mrs. Wilson and Mrs. Takahashi. I knew I was taking some advantage of my grandmother's hospitality, but I wanted to be there for their talk, wanted it so badly that I thought for the briefest moment I might not survive being excluded.

Mrs. Takahashi did not even question my invitation. "Your grandmother's?" she said simply. "That would be very nice."

9

WHEN HE WAS YOUNGER IT HAD ALWAYS BEEN HE AND JIMMY together—two boys, thin, tan, shirtless, wandering the hills until their minds were great topographical maps upon which were inscribed that esoteric hierarchy of meaning important to boys alone: the prime locales for fishing and swimming, the decayed oak husks that provided homes to rattlesnakes, the trees that could be most easily scaled, and the sources of the coldest, clearest water. There had been chores, too, of course, but in his memory there were long periods of adventure where they hiked the ridges and hills seemingly without end. But Ray was no longer a boy, and his thoughts, his very memories, had turned to ash and shadow. Now his waking dreams brought to mind not the innocence of boyhood, however lost, but what had come after: her face, her body, so often in his thoughts that he sometimes imagined he could actually feel the warmth of her flesh in his hands. Even his sleep was broken by the myth of a past that was already lost to him, although he did not yet know it.

On the way north they had watched Mount Shasta rotate across the windows of the train, its great hulking shape a silver ghost floating in the distant pines. Ray's father had begun speaking in Japanese at the sight of that mountain, almost as if he had locked into a kind of prayer, his voice wistful and lonely. When Ray asked him what he was saying his mother whispered to quiet him. What he could understand—and his understanding of Japanese was poor at best—was something about the mountain his father called Fujisan, a peak that Ray knew had risen above his father's home in Japan. He had known his father to be ever-practical, but now the man seemed enraptured to a fugue state, staring out toward that mountain, his view broken from time to time by a forest that seemed to rush in on the windows and then to flee into the distance.

Ray thought of Helen. He would have liked to tell her about this mountain, this mountain that had apparently reminded his father of another mountain, a Japanese mountain, and wondered if he could write her in such a way that she would understand that what he really wanted to tell her could never be written down. What he wanted—what he must have wanted—was a simple return to the way things had been before, and to that end he would have rolled the whole clock all the way back to his own childhood, before his heart had gone crazy, before his family had been sent off the only land he had ever known.

He sometimes thought of that great white peak in the long days after they arrived at Tule Lake: the barracks arranged in orderly rows, the fencing that enclosed them straight and clean, sagebrush rolling off in all directions, and the jagged line of Castle Rock rising against the southern sky. Beyond it, somewhere, was the white tower of Mount Shasta which he had come to think of as the ghost of his father's memory of Fujisan but which held no meaning to the son except that it lay in the general direction of home, a beacon he could not see for the desolate outcropping that stood in its path. He told himself that he would scale that desolation one day, perhaps soon, simply so that he could once more see what lay beyond it in the long stretch of the country to the southwest, the sugar pine and foxtail, cedars and firs and, once or twice along the road, oak trees like those that dotted the hills behind them. Here in the camp there were no trees at all.

The five of them shared one room, military-style cots crowding the tiny space. Sometimes his mother would have him stack those cots in a corner so that she could sweep the dust from the floor, although when the wind blew, and it blew nearly every day of the year, the dust swam through every crack and crevice despite the tar-paper siding, even blowing up through the gaps in the floor until each worn board was lined with a row of colorless soil. At first there had been no furniture at all except those cots—no shelves, no chests of drawers, no furniture upon and into which they might have unpacked their meager suitcases. But the War Relocation Authority would come by on occasion with scrap wood and he and the others would set to building what they needed. There were carpenters among them and someone set up a rudimentary shop, the tools mostly handmade, and from this and the labor of their own hands—Ray's and his father's—they built or acquired chairs and a kitchen table and shelves and a few cabinets from which his mother might produce a semblance of housekeeping. Later his father would procure a roll of used linoleum from a local farmer and they would move everything outside and his father kneel and push the roll across the boards until it was flat, a look of triumph in his eyes for which Ray was embarrassed, for what station had they reached that a roll of linoleum could serve as a triumph of the will?

Dear Helen & Jimmy, he wrote later that night. *It is lonely in this place but I am doing my best to keep my chin up. The room we are in is leaky as an old boat so dust blows in all the time. My dad put down some linoleum and I hope that helps some. Jimmy—are you in the Army now? I guess I won't be able to join. We could be storming Tokyo together. Maybe that sounds like a strange thing to say but that's how I feel about it. I know you do too. Helen—I hope you're well. We think of you guys here a lot. Nothing to do but think about things. Give my best to your mom and pop. —Ray*

———

EACH OF THE LETTERS they received from the Wilsons was almost identical to the one that had come before, as if the first had supplied a kind of blueprint. When Kimiko considered them later they seemed not unlike the rooms they were assigned at Tule Lake and later at Jerome: each a copy of the last. But the families had worked hard to build within the confines of their rooms a sense of the people within. The differences were small but they were significant enough to give those spaces at least the semblance of home, not for the Issei and perhaps not for the older of the Nisei either but for the children, at least for them. She had just come to understand this not long before I first met her when the older of her two granddaughters, age thirteen, had chosen to write a report on her family history. That child's mother, Doris, told her daughter what she recalled of those years—she had been eight at the start and eleven when the war had ended. It had not occurred to Doris that the girl would ask her grandmother and it would not have occurred to Doris that the girl's grandmother would speak of such things because never in Doris's life had her own mother so much as mentioned their time in the camps. "She answered your questions?" Doris stuttered. "Really?" and her daughter answered, "Sure she did. Why wouldn't she?" as if it were the most natural thing in the world. Doris read her daughter's notes later, notes which spoke to a variety of uncomplaining suffering that Doris herself found all too familiar, as if what had happened to her family were natural and could not be helped: the shared toilets, the barbed wire, the dust through the boards, the loss of their family home, all of it.

And yet it had not felt so badly to Doris herself at the time. One Sunday after church, when she and her mother sat in her living room in San Jose, she told her mother that it had not been so much like prison to her, nor, she surmised, to her sister Mary, but had been more like going on a kind of vacation, like camping. The children she knew were all assembled there together so that instead of only seeing her friends at the grammar school or at church on Sundays, she got to see them every day, and as there were few chores for children apart from homework, they were allowed to play together for hours and hours.

"But we had no choice," her mother had said in response, her hands, like soft paper now, held crossed upon her lap. "They put us there because they were afraid of us."

"I know," Doris said. She paused a long moment then. Her husband, a white man who sold electronic components and was often on the road, stood in the doorway listening, and Doris glanced up at him briefly before continuing. "I guess what I mean is that you did a good job," she said.

"Of what?"

"Of making us feel like everything was going to be all right. Block fifty-seven felt like home."

Kimiko exhaled sharply at this, her tone dismissive, her hands rising as if to wipe away the absurdity of such a statement. "It was a prison," she said. "Not home."

"I know, Mom," Doris said then. "I can't imagine what it was like for you. As a mother, I mean. I just wanted you to know that you did a good job of keeping things normal."

"Okasama, she's trying to give you a compliment." This from Doris's husband. He used the formal Japanese word for mother, something he did when he was trying to clamber past Kimiko's defenses, and while Kimiko herself recognized this ploy she could not help but smile inwardly at the man's care.

"I know," Kimiko said. "I know she is."

"It's not such a bad thing to be told you've done a good job," Doris's husband said now.

But she could say nothing to this. She had survived. Her husband had survived. Her daughters had survived. That was all.

———

IN MY GRANDMOTHER's living room, Mrs. Takahashi talked of the camps only sporadically, telling me—and sometimes Mrs. Wilson as well—what their lives had been like in that dismal shadscale desert in the far north of the state. Her granddaughter's school paper uncapped what had been, for decades, a period of Mrs. Takahashi's life which was simply not discussed, so that it might have felt to the generations to come after as if their parents and grandparents had simply decided to move from one place to another in a manner identical to the way in which those same parents or grandparents or great-grandparents had once decided to emigrate from Japan. She had not treated it quite as a secret or as something to be ashamed of but instead considered it under the wide umbrella of what she called, in passing, gaman.

"What did you call it?" I asked her when she sat upon my grandmother's settee on that warm summer afternoon, a fan buzzing from the corner. She had said the word twice or three times before, not offering enough pause afterwards for me to interrupt.

"It means to suffer in patience." A pause. Then: "To endure what you cannot control."

All these years later that term has stuck with me because it seems to embody a kind of silence that I felt I could understand, a silence that Chiggers had touched on when we sat together on my grandmother's porch in the night. I knew that what Mrs. Takahashi had told me did not really apply to my situation, for I had been a solider and had chosen to do what I had done, and yet the idea of it rang in my heart like a bell. To endure what you cannot control. That felt like everything I had returned to after the war. There are times today when it still does.

Mrs. Wilson looked shaken as she sat in that room, although sometimes I wondered if that was more my imagination than anything else, for she also continued to hold fast to the same steely resolve that encased her always. I had taken my grandmother's rattling sedan to retrieve her the moment my grandmother and Mrs. Takahashi fell into conversation, relying on my grandmother's directions to the Wilsons'. What I found was a house much

smaller than my childhood memories suggested, a somewhat taw-
dry Victorian in need of repair standing just at the top of Ridge
Road in a grove of twisted pear trees of great age, between which
the grass was high and unkempt. I was relieved to see the Pontiac parked there in the small gravel turnaround and I pulled my
grandmother's coughing sedan to a stop beside it and opened the
door to find that Mrs. Wilson had already appeared, her figure
upon the porch complete and ready as if she expected company,
a state of preparedness she always maintained as a mark of pride,
even in the relative country wilderness of central Placer County.

———

"HELEN'S BABY," MRS. TAKAHASHI said now. "That was why
you didn't want us to come back." It was not a question. Mrs.
Takahashi's brown eyes peered across to where Mrs. Wilson sat,
hands folded together upon her lap.

My grandmother's appearances and disappearances into
the kitchen for refreshments had settled into the relative distance of the room's opposite corner. She was not willing to
absent herself from the scene as she had when Chiggers had
come but was seemingly aware of the privacy needed. If Mrs.
Wilson still cared about the fact that her secret was becoming,
with each sentence shared in my grandmother's presence, no
secret at all, she did not express it, although once or twice I
thought I might have perceived a slight glance in my grandmother's direction.

"Yes, that's why," Mrs. Wilson said.

"I wish we would have known," Mrs. Takahashi said.

"I couldn't do that."

"Why?"

"You know why."

"Because we're Japanese."

She said nothing in response, did not nod, did not even move, her stare unwavering.

"We didn't understand," Mrs. Takahashi said now. "Hiro . . . he was so hurt."

"So was Homer," Mrs. Wilson said then.

"But Homer knew what was happening. He knew. Hiro didn't. What was he supposed to think?"

"He still felt terrible," Mrs. Wilson said. "Tak—Hiro, I mean—was his best friend."

"This is how he treats his best friend?"

Silence now, Mrs. Wilson looking first at Mrs. Takahashi and then to my grandmother and finally to me. "I didn't come here to be abused," she said then.

She rose to her feet and I with her and it was me who asked her to wait, told her to. "She came all this way," I said.

"Then she wasted her time."

"No she didn't," I said. "Just wait a minute. Please." I cannot explain why but I felt the first sharp wave of panic creeping into my heart, as if her departure from this house would have consequences detrimental to us all.

"Evelyn," Mrs. Takahashi said from the settee. "Please don't leave."

"Well, you're just . . . ," Mrs. Wilson began, her mouth opening and closing and opening once more as she started over: "I can't change what happened," she said. "I just can't."

"I know."

"We were all hurt by it, you know. Not just you."

"I know that too," Mrs. Takahashi said. "Please sit with me."

Mrs. Wilson was reluctant but at last she did so, her frame lowering itself in a manner almost robotic, a slow fluidity that brought her back to the edge of the sofa, her hands once again together in her lap.

"Will you help me?" Mrs. Takahashi said then.

"With what, Kim?"

"To find out what happened to my boy."

"Oh," Mrs. Wilson said. "Is that why you came?"

"Yes," she said. "That is why I came."

———

THE LETTERS SENT TO THEM in the camp were addressed to Hiroshi Takahashi, small envelopes containing a single sheet of plain white paper scribbled over in Homer's blocky script and filled with misspellings and awkward untutored phrasings that sometimes passed so close to humor that Hiro would often laugh as he read them, realizing, perhaps for the first time, that his own English was better than that of his American friend. Hiro would read the words once or twice in silence while the rest of them waited, the girls with increasing impatience (although the letters rarely included anything of interest to them at all), Ray with some measure of despondency, and Kimiko simply watching her husband's expression, the change between concentration and amusement and confusion that passed over his features like low clouds over the saltbush and sandy loam.

Hiro would then pass the letter to his eldest for reading aloud and Ray, already standing, would do so carefully, in a voice just loud enough for them all to hear, although of course they knew that the Hosokawas were very likely listening from the other side of the wall that incompletely divided their living quarters from that of their neighbors.

"Dear Tak and family," Ray might read. "We are fine here, but we miss our . . . fiends . . . oh, *friends*, he meant *friends*," and Hiro would chuckle. "We hope you are well. The peaches are all picked now and the pears too. We hired some people from Oklahoma who came through town. Most of the orchards had to since there are not enough pickers to go around now. It's hard to be a foreman. I'm sure you're not surprised to hear me say that," the vague, pointless chatter proceeding apace for a paragraph or so before dwindling and finally dying out like a lamp wick scorched down to its brass burner.

There was a lightness to the letters and it was that lightness that brought a smile to Hiro's face, but there was another facet which only Kimiko herself seemed aware of—the effect each had on her only son. She had long felt that something was bothering him, some constant darkness somehow more apparent each time a letter appeared from Newcastle. These were the moments in which he seemed to struggle the hardest to hide his heart, the play of that faint secret torment drifting over his features like the leaden clouds that sometimes came flooding over the desert, blackening the sage and pressing down upon Castle Rock. Sometimes she would watch him watching his father silently read through Homer Wilson's words and, were he to notice her watching him, his expression would change into a kind of mask. What had been—she was almost sure of it— deep and impenetrable sorrow would become, instead, a kind of stoniness, as if he had pressed whatever he had been feeling down into the well of his own heart and had, at least for the moment, managed to lock it away. It was something she herself had learned to do, but she was thirty-nine and was a wife and mother to three children and he was but nineteen. Hiro and the girls had been quick to adapt to the situation. Only Ray seemed to hold fast to the bleak truth of it. And herself. She knew, of course, that she too had trouble letting go.

"Tell me what's wrong," she said to him one night, during a rare moment when they were alone in the little room. A typically bland letter had arrived from the Wilsons (or rather from Homer, for none of the others ever sent any word to them at all). The girls had gone out soon after the reading and Hiro had wandered out in their wake, already tapping his pipe against his palm. She knew that Ray too would leave the room in a moment, following them into the failing day, the light planing down to such an angle that it seemed to skate along the blasted surface of the desert like a stone skipping on the flat of a pond. She wondered where he went, her eldest, her only boy, his thoughts already an enigma to her. Had that always been the case or had she lost him somewhere along the way?

"I'm fine, Mom," he told her.

"I know you," she said. "I know when you're fine."

He did not say what she thought he would, did not tell her again that he was "fine" or "all right" or "okay" or any of the other bland Americanisms that made her feel like she was talking to the radio rather than her flesh and blood. "It's just that . . . ," he began, pausing for a moment and then saying, "It's just that I kinda thought Jimmy and Helen might, you know, write to us too once in a while."

"You miss your friends," she said.

"Sure," he said.

"Maybe their father doesn't want them to?"

"Why wouldn't he?"

She shrugged. "Embarrassed. I don't know."

"Why would he be embarrassed?"

"I don't really have to answer that for you, do I?" she said.

"But she's—" He cut himself off, starting again with a kind of choking that his mother did not recognize at first but then saw for what it was: her son (her grown son, a man) was on the verge of tears. "I mean they're, you know, my best friends."

"You said *she*," his mother said then.

"What?"

"You said *she* at first. That's what you said."

"I just meant both of them."

"Did you?"

Then he said something so quietly that she had to lean in to catch his words and even then, when he repeated them, they were but a blur of sound.

"I want to go home." Then he was up out of the chair and out the door.

She called his name but he was already gone and she was alone again. She pulled out one of the chairs and sat at the edge of the table, one callused hand on its surface, the other in the lap of her worn dress. August. They had only been in the camp for three months, three months in which she had tried to grow accustomed to the fence and the shared toilets and meals in the dining hall, her life suddenly part of a communal whole with women she hardly knew or did not know at all, the dividing wall not reaching the ceiling so that every conversation of the neighboring family, the Hosokawas, could be heard, word for word, every argument, every discussion, even those rare moments of their lovemaking late at night. In the toilets she had to do what her body demanded seated next to whomever happened to be there, divided only by a flimsy cloth sheet hung on a drooping line so that the sounds and smells from the woman beside her mingled with her own. Each time the experience was horrifying and demeaning. Once she heard the sound of weeping from beyond the cloth sheet and through the gap could see an elderly woman whose name she did not know, her stained underwear pooled around her heels as her naked buttocks strained against the seat. Kimiko said nothing, for what could she say, instead moving past that woman and past another and lowering herself in disgust and shame.

She tried, a few days later, to talk to her husband about the shade that seemed to have entered their oldest child and which, as the days and weeks and months continued, would darken and coalesce into a kind of half-light, grim and silent. She did not actually believe Hiro might affect some change in the boy, or even that he was capable of discovering exactly what was on Ray's mind. She simply did not want to feel so wholly alone.

When she first introduced the topic, Hiro answered her with a proverb, a tactic he employed whenever he wanted to avoid a real conservation, and which never failed to irritate her. This time it was, "The caged bird dreams of clouds."

"Please be serious," she said in response.

"It's true, isn't it?"

"Just talk to him," she said, an edge to her voice now. "Find out what's wrong. Maybe there's something we can do."

Hiro did not look at her but instead cast his eyes out toward the little window with its uneven sheet of glass. "It's going to be sundown soon," he said, another evasion.

"Will you?"

For a long moment he did not move, but even in his stillness she knew he had heard her and when he nodded at last the action was so slight, so bare, that it was almost as if he had not moved at all.

"Good," she said. "Now go smoke your pipe."

He was a good man, her husband, but he was hardly a man to face a challenge head-on and in fact practiced a kind of active avoidance that she often found maddening even as she envied the skill. When they had first heard news of the Japanese attack on Pearl Harbor, Hiro's response had been to nod sadly, lift his coat from its hook, and set out on the path to the Wilsons'. She expected something from him in the morning at least, some acknowledgment that the world had changed, but he went out into the orchards as he always did and it was up to her to remove the little shrine, the photographs, the images and accoutrements of the life from which they had come, actions that she knew to be futile and yet what else could she do for her family but try to cover them in the pale paint of the country of their birth?

At certain times she had come to think of Hiro's steadiness as a kind of special power, for no matter what the situation he seemed unperturbed, perhaps even unperturbable. Even as they readied for departure to Tule Lake this was the case, his quiet sadness turning into simple resignation and to single-minded focus—they were leaving and had to prepare—a power that was

constant during all the years she had known him, right up until
that first September at Tule Lake when it broke all to pieces. It
was the final communication from the Wilsons that did it, a letter not even from the family itself but from a law firm neither
Hiro nor Kimiko had ever heard of before.

Hiroshi Takahashi, the letter began. *Your lease on the property of
Homer Wilson is hereby terminated effective immediately. Furthermore,
your personal goods stored at said location have been sold at auction to cover
expenses and rent past due. The net owed is zero. You are hereby forbidden
to contact Homer Wilson and his family in any way, shape or form. All
communication should be conducted through this office at the address listed.
Sincerely, Walter E. Shettley, Attorney-at-Law.*

Hiro did not tell her the contents of the letter the day of its
arrival nor the next nor the next, and he did not tell Ray until
the war was coming to an end and his return from Europe was
imminent. Even then he only relayed that Ray would not find
them in the hills of Newcastle but in Oakland, Hiro's own incredulity and confusion having been slowly evaporated until what
remained was simple endurance, gaman.

He did not tell Kimiko for three days, writing a letter to
Homer Wilson in the interim and posting it without her knowing, a simple document which was just as informal as any—
we are fine, Kimiko is fine, Ray is fine, Doris and Mary are
fine, letter arrived from unknown Walter E. Shettley, confusing,
etc.—and dropping it at the camp's post office and then thinking, believing, that when Homer's reply arrived it would confirm
what Hiro had decided almost immediately: that the letter had
been intended for someone else, that the hakujin lawyer, unfamiliar with Japanese names, had meant it to go to a Takamoto

or a Yamasashi, and while he could not determine what kind
of error had placed his own name both on the envelope and in
the letter itself he continued to believe that it had been an error.
He could not stop looking at the document, unfolding it on the
walks he sometimes made around the exterior of the grounds,
the fence scrolling by on his left and the letter often clutched in
his hand. He would occasionally nod at passersby, and some—
men he knew from the camp—even asked what he was reading,
what had drawn from him such an intense look of concentration. Each time he would make up some excuse or simply smile,
say, "Nothing of interest," and then ask them about their children, their wives.

He told himself that the whole of the letter had been a simple
error, and yet as the days passed he could not help but wonder
how such a thing could happen, how a lawyer could make a mistake that called both himself and Homer Wilson by name, an
error which could not be waved away as a simple bureaucratic
mistake. Then came the first warm flush of doubt, its surface as
hard and rough as a peach's stone pit. The light low in the west
so that the fence's shadow was written in a faintly wavering line
against the colorless dust.

He handed her the letter that night, the children gone from
the room, his wife lowering herself into one of the chairs at the
table, the letter in her hand, her eyes continuing to stare at its
lines of type, at the signature of the lawyer, Walter E. Shettley.

"It must be a mistake?" he said at last, the sentence curling
up into a question although it was, in fact, no question at all but
a kind of querulous statement of hope.

"No," she said quietly. "No mistake."

"But why?"

"You trusted them," she said.

"He's my friend."

And now, at last, she moved, her head snapping up from the table to stare at him, eyes bright and sharp and glaring. "Your friend? Your friend?"

He nodded. "He is my friend."

"He's hakujin," she said.

"He doesn't think like you do."

"Like I do? You think I make him hakujin? You think I do that?"

"Quiet now," Hiro said then. He flicked his chin in the direction of the neighbors.

"You're a foolish man."

"Don't," he said.

"I'm telling you the truth," she said. Then she said his name. She did not say it often, using instead Otōsan, Father, to reflect his role in the family. But she said it now, "Hiro." Then, "I know he was important to you."

"He's my friend."

Her eyes went to the letter again, reading it through once more. Then she folded it back into its little square. "You should burn this," she said.

"You think it's true?"

"How could it not be true?"

"A mistake."

"You know it's not a mistake."

For the rest of her life, she would remember how he looked in that moment, the mingling of despair and betrayal and fear passing across his features like the wind over a field of grass. How she wished she could pull him to her like she had seen in American moving pictures: two people crashing together with such power that it was as if they had become magnets drawn to each other alone. But she and Hiro did not have that kind of relationship. She did not know if anyone actually did.

"What will we do?" her husband said then.

"Find somewhere else."

"Where?"

"We'll find something," she said.

"I don't understand. I don't understand what happened. What could have happened?"

"Money maybe."

"He wouldn't do that."

"But he did. He is."

"Why? Why is this happening?"

"Because this is not our home."

"This isn't forever," he said. "This is just for now."

"I don't mean this place," Kimiko said then, gesturing at the walls, the floors, the sandblasted windows, the cooking stove.

It matters little if there were more words between them; those words would have been more of the same and they would have quieted after a time and Hiro would have folded the letter once more into his pocket and wandered outside with his pipe. She insisted that he needed his solitary walk, when in fact it was she herself who needed to be alone. The fact of that letter, of Walter E. Shettley's missive, washed over her like a wave, not its ultimate meaning—nearly three decades would pass before she truly understood what it all meant and even then her knowledge would be partial—but what it meant for her and Hiro and the children and what it might mean for Ray. She found herself seated not in the chair now but on the edge of Doris's bed, sitting on its lumpy edge and staring forward until the gaps in the wall boards faded into a wavering texture of soft horizontal stripes beyond which was the barbed-wired fence that held all the world: a flat bare space containing only humiliation and loneliness.

"Don't tell Raymond," she had told her husband before he left the room, pipe in hand. "Don't tell any of them but especially not Raymond."

"Of course I won't tell him."

"It would destroy him."

"He's tough."

"Just don't tell any of them."

"I won't," he said simply. And then he was outside and the door clacked closed behind him.

What she thought then was a kind of terrible relief. Everything was clear at last. The tenor of the words themselves—their style, their sparsity, the directness of their expression—had obliterated what she knew had been one of her husband's central beliefs: that they were, he and Homer Wilson, somehow equals, this despite the fact that Homer Wilson was white and an American citizen and a landowner and therefore part of the very fabric of the nation in a way that her husband and herself and their children could never be. Their internment was only the latest in a long series of differences that stacked one against the other from the moment she had been sold across the sea in the joint conspiracy between the matchmaker and her parents. Hiro had told the children that it was for their own good, that they might well have been physically attacked had they remained in Placer

County with the fervor of anti-Japanese sentiment roiling the air. What a naïve fool.

But she knew who she was. She was Japanese. That was how she thought of herself and knew she would continue to think of herself no matter how many years she lived in this country. She had understood this long before the buses had arrived and it had become plain to everyone who could call themselves Americans and who could not.

———

AND YET SHE HAD never been free of those hills with their rows of peach and plum and pear trees and the golden grasses and olive-colored oaks and the blaze of summer heat coming up from the earth. For twenty-seven years she would be away from that landscape but her memories of her son would be forever entangled in that same topography so that she could not think of him without thinking of the oaks and the orchards and their little house on its hill and the big white Victorian of the Wilsons' on the hill opposite and the little town with its fruit sheds and the tumbledown buildings of the little Japantown that nestled in the draw at the foot of Chantry Hill. Her boy. Her beautiful boy. There he had been and then the war came and then Tule Lake and Raymond had gone to war as a soldier then had simply vanished, gone so completely that it sometimes felt as if his entire existence had been a kind of hallucination or vision. For a long while she had felt in her heart that he yet lived and had decided, for reasons she could not fathom, to remain apart from his family—from his mother and father and sisters—but the years passed and then it was 1950 and 1955 and she knew that her son was dead, knew it and had even come to accept it in the warm beating center of her heart.

And then she understood something she had not even asked of herself, knew that Evelyn Wilson too was a survivor, that she too was a mother of the dead.

"Help me, Evelyn," she said now. "Please, help me."

I had drawn myself up to the edge of my seat and a quick glance to my grandmother confirmed that she had as well, the two of us suspended there in anticipation of Evelyn Wilson's response. Evelyn Wilson herself betrayed nothing of her own thoughts, her face emotionless, seeming to suspend our expectation not out of malice but out of utter indifference.

When at last she spoke her voice seemed to come from that same indifference, her words uttered as if they were the only answer possible. Only later did I come to understand that she did it not out of the goodness of her heart but out of a sincere desire for control, assuming as she did—and rightly—that Mrs. Takahashi would not simply return to San Jose unappeased.

"Yes," she said finally. "Of course I'll help you, Kim. Of course I will."

10

IT WOULD TAKE NEARLY A MONTH BEFORE THE IMPLICATIONS
of Mrs. Wilson's agreement to help Mrs. Takahashi were fully
understood, namely that her own culpability was more central to
the narrative than at first appeared. She herself was unaware—
and would be unaware for all her life—just how much she was to
blame, but at that time we were grateful for any sense of guidance. Mrs. Wilson had been there in the county in 1945 and had
seen Ray—had seen him, we still thought, only at a distance in
Auburn—and so was the first point of contact we had with any
kind of tangible information. Mrs. Wilson had agreed to help
Mrs. Takahashi, after all, and even told her she would meet her
there at my grandmother's whenever Mrs. Takahashi wanted to
make the drive up from San Jose, which she did six times over
the next five weeks. Each time, Mrs. Wilson would appear at
my grandmother's soon after Mrs. Takahashi's arrival and my
grandmother would offer them tea, then they would both take
their seats in Mrs. Wilson's Pontiac: Mrs. Takahashi in the back,

Mrs. Wilson in the passenger seat, and I the driver. (I made some excuse to the filling station's owner on these afternoons, telling him that I had to help drive an elderly relative about for some appointments and did not entirely know when such an errand would end. Mr. Borton, for his part, was irritated only to the extent that my absence meant he would need to be at the filling station office in my stead. By the end of the intrigues with Mrs. Wilson and Mrs. Takahashi, I determined that my life was better spent elsewhere and convinced Mr. Borton to reduce my employment to part-time so I might take advantage of the G.I. Bill at the local community college. It took me eight years to complete my college and university education, but I graduated at last with a master's degree in 1977, having published the first of several novels.)

I will not belabor you with the various witnesses we spoke to over those weeks, witnesses who described days wholly unremarkable and which we cobbled together from the vague reminiscences of people who often could hardly remember Ray Takahashi at all. "Oh yeah, right, right, I think I do remember him," one might say. "I think I saw him once at the picture show over in Auburn" or "Yeah, yeah, saw him once at the drugstore there in Loomis, eating a sundae at the counter I think. No I don't think anyone was with him," or something similar. Most such reminiscences were mundane and pointless, but one or two carried with them a fresh stab. An old Japanese farmer in Loomis recalled Mr. Takahashi contacting him in search of news, and then further remembered seeing Raymond in the flesh a few weeks later, head down, walking up Ridge Road from the irrigation canal. The farmer had pulled over and asked Ray if he needed a ride and Ray had told him that he did not and then the farmer had told the young soldier that his father had been in touch looking for him and that he should call or write home right away. Ray nodded and said he would use the public phone in town and that anyway he had just been home and that his parents knew of his whereabouts and all was well. "That was all," the old farmer said with a shrug. "I think I only saw him that one time, walking up the road like that."

"My God, Kim," Mrs. Wilson said after we had driven away, back downhill, back toward the old highway. "It's almost too much to bear. It's almost too much," her own incredulity seemingly as profound and troubled as that of Mrs. Takahashi herself. (Toward the end of that period, when summer had broken to a cold wet autumn, Mrs. Wilson's reaction was revealed to be merely relief at another dead end in which she was not implicated. But there was to be a final piece of the story yet to come in the figure of Jim Tuttle, young son of the Oklahoma family who were the only other tenants of the little whitewashed box that was still thought of as the Takahashi home. After nearly everyone in the story was dead, my grandmother first, then Mrs. Takahashi, and finally Mrs. Wilson herself, leaving only me and the teller, he would appear out of nowhere on a hot still summer afternoon in 1983 and at last offer the nearest thing to closure this story can ever have.)

Towards the end of that period, Mrs. Takahashi asked me to drive us to nearby Penryn to visit the Buddhist church, Mrs. Wilson having, during their earliest conversations, suggested that Ray might have slept there.

I expected something with a spire and stained glass, if only because that was what the word "church" meant to me, but the church to which I was directed was a plain, plaster-covered residential house, converted to its current use many decades before. Twenty-seven years had passed since Mrs. Takahashi had last set foot inside its cool, dark interior, but that central room had remained unchanged: smelling of incense and polished wood and carrying, in its shadows, a peaceful quietude. The pews looked not unlike those of the various Catholic churches of my childhood, although in place of some bleeding Jesus at the head of the room was a kind of altar or shrine carved from dark teak upon which sat the image of the Buddha surrounded by various incense containers, small books, gongs, and the like.

When the priest appeared, he and Mrs. Takahashi exchanged greetings in Japanese. He was a diminutive man, bald and very old, and he smiled warmly in my direction when Mrs. Takahashi introduced me. The conversation continued in Japanese, so that I knew nothing of what was said and eventually excused myself, returning to the blazing heat of the parking lot.

"Did she find someone to talk to?" Evelyn Wilson asked me. She had remained in the passenger seat, window rolled down, and if she perspired at all there was no indication of it.

"She's talking to the priest," I said. "Is he a priest? I'm not sure that's the right word."

"I don't know," she said. "Thank you for driving us around. I'm sure there are things you'd rather be doing."

"Not really," I said.

"What are your friends doing?"

"I don't know anyone around here, really," I said. "Just my gran."

"Is that what you call her? Your gran?"

"That's what I've always called her. You're a . . . I mean, you've got grandchildren, right?"

She did not answer for a time, her eyes, behind those great orb-like sunglasses, staring out past me into the bright summer sunlight. Then she said, "Yes, I've got grandchildren."

"What do they call you?"

"I don't know," she said. "They don't call me anything."

"What do you mean?"

"I don't have a relationship with them."

"Oh," I said. "I'm sorry. I didn't mean to . . . I mean . . . boy, I just stepped in it, didn't I?"

"It's all right," she said. "My daughter Helen, her husband's from Chicago and they both moved out there. Helen and I, well, we just don't have a relationship." She shook her head. "It's one of the reasons I finally got up the courage to go talk to Kim. I thought if I could find her son then maybe I could find my grandson."

"Because he's the only grandchild you have left."

"He's the only one I have left at all," she said then. "My husband's gone. Heart failure, of all things, which is ironic since the man had the biggest heart of anyone I ever knew. You know, for a while I blamed Ray for that too."

"How's that?"

"I thought he sullied my daughter's honor. That Ray did, I mean. It sounds so old-fashioned now. And when I went up to Seattle to take care of the problem—to have the problem taken care of, I mean—well, I don't think my husband ever really forgave me for that."

"He had to understand it though. Didn't he?"

"I don't know. Tak really was my husband's best friend in all the world. I didn't really think it was possible even back then. I mean I didn't think it was possible that he could overlook the fact that Tak was Japanese. It just seemed like too much."

"But don't you have a son too?"

"Oh," she said sadly, "that'd be Jimmy."

I waited for her to say more but the church's door had opened and Mrs. Takahashi appeared, the priest just behind her, the two of them turning toward each other and bowing slightly, saying something that I could not hear. Mrs. Takahashi stepped down to the gravel of the parking lot and then to the car.

"What'd he say, Kim?" Mrs. Wilson asked her as I moved to the driver's seat once more.

Mrs. Takahashi did not answer until I had pulled the car out onto the road again. When at last she spoke, her voice was hardly audible at all. "He was here," she said. "Raymond was here."

"He remembered that?" Mrs. Wilson said.

"He remembered my family. And he remembered my husband coming to look for Raymond."

"What'd he say?"

"He said that Raymond arrived soon after my husband did. Days or weeks. And Raymond told the priest that he'd already been home. The priest was satisfied. So that was the end of his concern."

It had been the same everywhere then, Raymond's invisible presence in Placer County being predicated on simple trust. He said he had been home—home, that is, to Oakland—and this was taken as fact and no further thought was given to contacting his family.

"I'm sorry, Kim," Mrs. Wilson said.

"He slept here."

"Every night?" I asked.

"Almost every night," she said. "That's what he told me."

It was silent in the car for a time. I kept waiting for either of them to comment on what was, at least to me, the obvious question, but when neither of them spoke again, I finally asked it: "Where was he those other nights?"

"What do you mean?" Mrs. Wilson said from beside me.

"The priest said he slept there almost every night. So where did he sleep when he wasn't at the church?"

"Outside," Mrs. Takahashi said from the backseat.

"Outside?"

"He said outside. I think I know where."

"Where?"

"I'll show you," she said, and when the road split she murmured to take the fork to the left and I did so, the car's great wide hood rocking over the brief hot undulation in the asphalt roadbed.

———

THE PLACE TO WHICH Mrs. Takahashi directed us might not have been so very far from the old house in which she had lived on the Wilson property, but it felt, along the winding roads of the outskirts of the county, as if it were some secret place. The road ran alongside a ridge so tangled with vegetation that at times it arched over the path so that the Pontiac pointed on through a verdant tunnel lined with summer sunlight that seemed to spark in the afternoon's heat. When at last we climbed into the open again it was to find ourselves at the top of a high, flat ridge upon which grew the rough and twisted shapes of oaks amidst pale boulders and waving runnels of golden grass.

"He would camp out here sometimes," Mrs. Takahashi said. The only sounds, once I had shut the car off, were of wind through leaves and stones and dry yellow stalks.

"Jimmy would too," Mrs. Wilson said.

I stepped out and walked a few dozen yards into the grass. That he had camped here after his return from the war felt real to me in a way that the other locations we had visited did not, real in the sense that I could, for the first time, feel his presence, feel that he had existed in flesh and bone and blood. He had walked here and had ideas and thoughts and desires. Why I felt him in that place, upon that ridge, I cannot explain any more than I can explain why I felt or still feel that it is my responsibility to tell any of this story at all, but upon that ridge I could understand why someone might come here with a friend, with a lover, or even with the sounds and sensations of war still rattling in his chest, seeking grace and perhaps even absolution as if still a soldier, his body wrapped in his greatcoat, the grasses flattened into a circle around him so that the still-vertical perimeter of their untangled stalks seemed a wall to shelter him from enemy soldiers or gunfire or mortar shells. For we had learned this much, he and I, that to sleep at all was a luxury, and to sleep without death's constant stalking presence was an almost inconceivable extravagance.

The idea that Ray might yet be alive had seemed impossible to me, at least until I stood upon that ridge in the afternoon, the two women remaining in the car beside the road as I stood in the shade of an oak, staring out at the grass that rolled in shaking waves when the faint hot breeze ruffled the fringes of my hair. How he must have dreamed of her here, maddening close, the house in which she lay hidden just atop the next ridge. But for all that proximity she might as well have been in Italy or France or Japan. Everything was the same and yet everything had gone crazy. What a thing, to be confronted by the foreman on the same property upon which he had spent all his life. What a strange, foreign world he had returned to, as if in fighting for America he had only brought to the fore those aspects of his country that had previously been held in embarrassed secrecy. Or maybe that was not true either; maybe he had simply been too young to notice, to understand his own difference, his body the betrayer because he was and ever would be Japanese no matter how many wars he fought for the country of his birth.

You get away from me. You get off my porch. Go on! Get off my porch! I don't want you coming near this family. Do you hear me? Do you? Just get away. Get away.

He must have seen immediately that it had not been a misunderstanding, although of course he still did not know why. Perhaps his relationship with Helen might have been discovered or, an even more fleeting thought, perhaps she had been with child. The thought of such a pregnancy, the very idea of it, would turn his gut over with such fury and terror that his mouth would water in anticipation of vomiting. It could not have been that. Helen would tell him the truth. Or Jimmy would. Perhaps he would simply wait on the steps until one of them appeared. And this was essentially what he would try to do for the next three days, until the Wilsons hired a group of men to guard the road and to drive him away before he could even step onto the property, a fact I would learn at the same time I would learn the rest of what the Wilsons had done to Ray.

———

I CAME UP TO THE RIDGE many times afterwards, well after summer was gone and the whole of the ridgetop pressed closer to the sky, its countenance graying over with cloud cover and then, later still, watching it awake from that winter slumber. All through that period there was evidence of youth amidst the grasses: the black ring of a campfire, a loose sock and discarded condom, empty beer bottles: secrets of youth which are, of course, secrets to no one, ownership extending on into perpetuity to whatever generation might come after just as they had presumably been inherited from whatever generation had come before.

So that was where he and Helen had—what? fallen in love? made love?—perhaps all of it. It might have happened in an instant, him realizing (or had it been her?) that she was no longer a child, no longer simply the little sister of his best friend. And with that understanding would have come another, sharper understanding, which was that he was, in fact, different from them in ways which he had ignored or had tried to ignore for all the days of his life. Perhaps he should have seen this from the beginning, but it did not really reach his conscious mind until the days of Helen, days in which the very color of the world seemed to shift and change. The bright aurora of his childhood was honeyed by the sense of her, by the smell of her skin, deepened and darkened until everything in his life seemed lined with contrast, each bright shining moment ringed in aphotic and shadowed silhouette. He could not have traced how it had happened and even when he knew it had, knew that he had fallen in love with her—with Helen of all people!—he still could not trace its shape.

There must have been this or something very like it: a night at the ridge when he and Jimmy and a few others had built a small campfire on a damp evening, the sun dropping early and the whole world hushing around them. One of the other boys had brought a six-pack of beer and they each had one. Helen had come with them at her own insistence; Jimmy was nineteen now and had graduated from high school—Ray too—and Helen was but sixteen and Jimmy had grown tired of dragging his kid sister around, and yet she had managed to talk him into it and had arrived to find a few other boys and girls already there, all of whom were older than she was by three years or more.

He did not know if it was the desire of the other boys that drew him to her; the thought that his desire was so easily swayed was embarrassing and yet it had been clear that night that Helen had crossed some invisible line into womanhood. The other boys at the campfire watched her and talked with her and laughed when she laughed. Jimmy seemed oblivious to the change but Ray was not. Nor was Helen. She was like a diamond that night, funny and captivating and very much older than her sixteen years. Several times across the heat and orange glow of the campfire, her eyes locked with Ray's. The first time he looked away just at the moment of that invisible impossible touch, and when he glanced back again she had already moved on, leaning in now to listen to something Hank Pinkerton was whispering in her ear. The next time she looked in Ray's direction he held her gaze, their eyes meeting somewhere in that tumult of flame heat. It was she who broke the contact that time and afterwards he was left with a feeling so unfamiliar, so strange and awful and wonderful all at once, that he had trouble regaining his breath; it was, indeed, as if the whole of his being had been interrupted.

He could not understand what had happened at the campfire even though it was all he thought about during the drive back to the Wilsons', Helen's leg and hip pressed against his own, she and Jimmy chattering about something he was not listening to until Jimmy called to him across the cab of the truck in the sing-song faux-Asian voice he sometimes adopted when wanting to seem less serious than he actually was: "Hey why you so quiet, Charlie Chan?"

"Just tired out, I guess," Ray said, exhaling.

"You so lazy," Jimmy said. "You go night-night. Get some sleepy-sleeps."

"Right," Ray said.

"Something on your mind, Ray?" This was Helen now, her voice sounding different than it ever had, than it ever would again, not bright or loud or anything but mellow and quiet and soft.

"Nothing I can think of," Ray said in response.

Later they parked the truck at the Wilsons' and Jimmy and Helen stepped out and Jimmy said, "See ya," and Helen waved and then they were gone and Ray stood in the darkness alone, staring first at the house and then at the silvery shape of the trail that led through the orchard rows from this home to that of his own family, still wondering at what point Helen had grown up and why he had not noticed it before. The night around him alive with insect sounds and the fluttering singing of tiny frogs. There under the bright purple dome of the stars.

At some other time, in some other world than this, they might have merely looked at each other across one campfire or another and understood, simply and plainly, that they were not meant for each other, clearly seeing each other that one time and then moving on to other people, other friends, other lovers. But then the order had been announced and the world itself changed all at once into a kind of crucible.

Jimmy appeared at their little whitewashed home that day, the day they all heard the news, their fathers already bowed head-to-head in conversation, expressions serious and words hushed. Ray and Jimmy left them to it, walking down the hill through trees damp with February rain, Jimmy chattering much as Mr. Wilson had been back at the house, expressing his outrage and his belief, a belief he would continue to hold, that it would all come to nothing.

"I'm sure you're right," Ray told him in response.

"I am. I know I am. Hell, Ray, we're gonna join the army together, right?"

"Sure we are, Jimmy," he said. He wondered, not for the first time that day, where Helen was. "We'll show those Japs."

"Ha!" Jimmy said. "Good one, Ray. Those Japs! Yeah, those Japs! We'll show 'em for sure."

Helen did not come that day nor the next nor even the day after that, although he hoped and feared that she would. The night of the campfire was months in the past now, and he sometimes thought that the whole thing had been a kind of hallucination. But there had been moments since that night, unspoken moments between them when he saw her staring back at him through the trees or across the dinner table when he supped with the Wilsons, glances so quick and furtive that he wondered if they had occurred at all.

———

SHE CAME TO HIM at last during the fierce spring gloaming one late afternoon in early March. He had not seen her at all in over a month and had just begun to wonder why she would choose to avoid him, and why now, of all times. But maybe he was imagining the whole thing, his desire to see her, to simply see her, making her absence acute and meaningful, where before he might not have noticed her absence at all.

He had been working on the truck with Jimmy that day and they had cleaned up at the outdoor spigot and Ray had come down the hill path toward his own home. He could see his sisters through the trees: Mary on the tire swing he and Jimmy had hung from the branches of the persimmon in the dooryard; Doris just beside her. The sun was dropping and the orchard was mostly in shadow. He knew that, from either house, the path was but a darkness now. And it was into this darkness that she came, first saying his name so that he stopped and turned and peered at her there on the shadowed path, the sky still bright above them and the whole world below a silhouette.

"Ray?"

The voice was so quiet, so breathless, that it took him a moment to realize that it had not simply been a facet of his pining imagination. But no no yes there she was, standing in the shadows with stripes of blue moonlight crossing the thin shape of her body.

"What are you doing out here?" he said.

"I just wanted to tell you . . . ," she said, stopping now.

"What is it?"

She stepped toward him. He could not move, his hands at his sides even as she came to him, a few feet apart, then less. He had not realized that she was, at sixteen, an inch taller than him, so that he had to look slightly upwards to meet her eyes.

"I don't want you to go."

"I don't want to go either," he said simply.

But then she was crying and because he did not know what else to do he reached across those last few inches and pulled her to him and their arms encircled each other. His hand on the back of her head. His fingers in her yellow hair. Even in the moonlight it was like gold. His voice softly shushing her. "Everything'll be fine, Helen," he said. "Everything's going to be fine."

He thought he could feel her heart beating against him, its shape somewhere amidst the pressure of her breasts, the heat of her.

"God, Ray," she said. "Why is this happening?"

"I don't know," he said.

She stood pressed against him for another moment, a moment in which the night orchard all around them hissed and hummed and scraped and rattled in its quiet way. When she pulled her head away from his chest he thought she meant to break the embrace but then her lips were on his own, a quick, soft kiss. And then she turned and fled back along the trail toward the great dark silhouette of the Wilsons' house. He stood for a long while in the night under the shadows of the first rows of trees, watching until the light of the room he knew to be Helen's lit up from inside, a yellow rectangle cut there into the firmament of a million wheeling stars.

Months would pass before he would lie with her on a scratchy woolen blanket unfolded upon the broken yellow grasses below a similar sky and she would love him. They would love each other. In secrecy and in silence. And then all of it would blow away, not only because of history but because of their very lives, adrift as they were in the swirling spinning sea between one continent and another.

———

THE BUSES CAME two months later, a scene you have already watched unfold but which I give you again because it was the last time they were all three together. Look at them there—Ray and Jimmy and Helen—in their tight knot upon the gravel, leaning together, Jimmy having just announced his own big secret, that he had signed up for the army three days before, this news very nearly buckling Ray to his knees. He wished, indeed, that Jimmy had not told him at all. His friend would go off to fight in the war and Ray would—what?—be stuck with his family in some place he had never heard of. But of course he did not say any of this. Instead he looked to the dust at his feet and said something about how angry Jimmy's father would be when he heard the news.

Helen's voice then: "I'll say."

And Ray did not look toward the sound, kept his eyes on the neutral ground at their feet.

"There's nothing he can do about it now," Jimmy said. "I'm property of Uncle Sam."

"Won't he need you?"

"Shoot, Ray," Jimmy said. "You're supposed to be on my dang side."

"I am."

"Are you?"

Ray looked up now. Jimmy was, like his father, a head taller than Ray, gangly and slightly bucktoothed, freckled and bearing too his father's great pink ears.

"Jeez, Jimmy," Helen said.

"I said I was sorry."

"You did not."

"Well, I am."

"That's helpful."

"Can it, Helen," Jimmy said.

"Oh don't look so blue, Ray," Helen said then. Her foot in the gravel, the thin shape of it, came forward now and poked at his own shoe, its pale, dirty toe.

"I'm all right," he said.

"You'll come back," she said.

Still he could not raise his head to look at her.

"It won't be so bad. Just think of it as an adventure."

"That's right," Jimmy said. "We'll keep all your stuff together. Mom and Dad said so. So don't worry."

"Ray?" she said now.

"What?"

"Are you even listening?"

"Sure I am," he said.

"Well, why don't you look at me?"

Mr. Wilson's voice came then, a short sound across the stacked parcels and the gravel. Jimmy turned and went toward his father and then they were alone, just the two of them, still in the square with everyone else and yet alone as he hoped and feared they would be, if only for the briefest moment.

"Look at me, Ray," Helen said.

And now he did so at long last, although it took all of his effort to keep from breaking to pieces in the process, her ankles and the bare flesh of her calves and then her legs obscured by the plaid skirt she wore and then the shape of her waist at its top, the faint swell of her breasts, her arms loose at her sides in their sleeves of white fabric. When his eyes had finished the lap of her body her gaze felt a lance or bayonet that seemed to cleave directly into his heart.

"Ray," she said, her voice a whisper. "You won't forget me, will you?"

"My God," he said. "Of course I won't. I wouldn't. I *can't*."

"Shake my hand," she said.

"What?"

She held her hand out to him now, suspended in the air before him. "Just do it," she said.

He raised his hand and she clasped it as if she were concluding some business of which he was unaware. But then he felt it: a small, round object that fit into his palm, something cold and hard and smooth.

"Don't look at it now," she said. "Just put it in your pocket."

The sound that came up the old highway was of the hard, high squeal of air brakes and then the rattle of a diesel engine. He realized he had been listening to the great beast roll toward them for a long while.

"They're coming," he said, and now his eyes went to hers.

"You'll be all right."

"I don't want to go."

"I know," she said. Her voice was breathless, a kind of wind, a hiss.

"Raymond? Raymond?"

He looked toward where his mother stood, his father beside her, the two of them flanked by the Wilsons. Jimmy stood just a few feet away, staring in the direction of Ray and Helen.

His father called to him to find his sisters and then waved a hand.

"I'll help," Helen said quietly.

He could feel a pull then at her words, a tingling in his lower gut that seemed to shake through him all at once.

"I'm gonna help," she called.

He thought that Jimmy might come then but Jimmy only stood there watching as they walked toward the sheds, their bodies dipping into the shadows, Ray feeling Jimmy's eyes on him even when he knew neither he nor Helen could be seen after they had rounded the corner of the sheds, the railroad tracks stretching off into the sunlight and not a soul in sight.

He pulled her to him then and their lips met, blooming darkly with blood and youth and fear. He could feel her tongue, could taste it on his own, slippery in the warm darkness of her mouth.

And then the voice of a child very close so that the two leapt apart as if from electric shock: "Ooh! Kissy kissy!"

The older of the Takahashi sisters stood just outside the shade, pointing and laughing. "Kissy kissy!" she said again.

"Mary!" Ray shouted. "You shut your mouth."

"Kissy kissy!"

He reached her before she could escape, his hand dragging her forward, his flat palm striking her face with a loud slap that elicited, from Helen, just behind him now, an audible gasp. "You shut your mouth, Mary!" he hissed.

"You hurt me!" the child squealed.

"I'll hurt you more if you tell anyone. You hear me?" She did not respond and he pulled hard on her arm again. "Do you?"

She nodded now, her tears flying fast down her cheeks.

"Where's your sister?"

"Let go of me!"

"Where's Doris?"

"At the bus," the little girl mumbled sullenly, still crying faintly so that her voice was high and twisted by her grief. "They sent me to find you, dumb head."

He stood for a moment, holding her there, frozen, the girl's face drooping toward the dirt and weeds. Then he said simply, "Go on then," and let her go.

"Ray," Helen said, her voice breathless. "You shouldn't have done that."

"What if she tells someone what she saw?"

"She won't. She wouldn't."

"She would. Those two are the biggest bunch of tattletales ever made."

They stood looking at each other then. "We should go back," he said.

That was all. Not, as it would turn out, their final meeting but the last time she would look at him as an object of her love, the end point of a long shining rope that, for a time, tied them together heart to heart. This image of them was hers, to hold her during whatever weeks and months were to come.

She did not know where the Takahashis were going, her father's answer to her question vague, without a place name or locator of any kind, nothing with which she might consult the Rand McNally. Their departure, not just of the Takahashis but of other of her classmates at the high school in Auburn, felt as if directed into a mystifying fog. If only she knew where they were going she might study it and think on it and investigate it in the library and so then she would know something and could tie one end of that shining rope around that place so that it would be held there in her heart like a stone.

But of course that moment behind the fruit sheds had really been the beginning of its end. That her heart would turn in the weeks and months and years to follow, that it would turn away from Raymond Takahashi and toward closer, more immediate possibilities would be surprising only in a novel, for how long could we expect a teenage heart to stay true across the waters of some unknown sea? Helen would pine for her first love for a few months and then she would be gone for much of the rest of the year. That part of the story I have already told. By the time Ray Takahashi appeared in Placer County in 1945 she had long since returned and had been seeing a local boy, the son of a machinist, for eleven months. She would not marry that boy and I do not think she had yet come to the conclusion that she had to leave the county altogether, had to find someone to marry who would take her away. That conclusion, I think, came later, when Ray happened upon her at a diner in Auburn and she understood at last that the carefully constructed artifice that

had become her life was not her own work at all but was and
had always been the work of her mother, and were she to live
she would need to flee everything she had ever known for some
brighter future elsewhere upon the globe.

———

THE SCENE AT THE DINER was one I learned of only because
Mrs. Wilson inadvertently referred to it during what might
have otherwise been a brief exchange upon parting. "It was
like he came back just to finish ruining what he had started
those years before," she told me that night in her Pontiac
after Mrs. Takahashi had left for San Jose. This was five
weeks after Mrs. Takahashi's first appearance at the filling
station, and we had met and driven around to various locations a half dozen times in the days between. We had discovered, frankly, very little that might lead us to understand
the situation which had resulted in Ray Takahashi's disappearance, although we did know something of his movements
during those weeks, twenty-seven years before, when he had
walked the hills of Placer County looking for answers he
would never find.

As it would turn out, the night of that conversation was
effectively the end of those days, when the two women and I
would drive along those snaking roads through the oaks and
the last of the orchards. The great teeming industry of Placer
County fruit production had been decimated, I was to learn,
by a statewide blight that killed off the trees even as the industry itself was faltering, that whole era coming to an abrupt

close within a span of a few agonizing months, the orchards dead, the sheds closed, the towns along the old highway never really recovering, so that what remained when I arrived were quaint collections of old-fashioned houses and touristy businesses huddled beside the constant roar of the new interstate. I did not know that that day in late summer was to be the last with Mrs. Wilson and Mrs. Takahashi, although thinking back on it now I might have surmised that the end was coming, for we had driven up and down the county looking for clues that were simply not there. July had broken into August and then August too was coming to a close.

That last day was not unlike all the days that had come before, a kind of pointless and meandering drive, unguided and unmapped, to find any scrap of information that yet remained. We had visited a corner drugstore in Loomis owned and operated by a Japanese-American family, one of the few that had returned to the area after internment. They greeted Ms. Takahashi in English, the proprietor gathering his wife and grandmother and children from the back room, all of them smiling and nodding. They recalled generally that Ray had been in the area in 1945, if only briefly, remembering him mostly because of his uniform, a uniform he was apparently never seen without.

When we left that drugstore, Mrs. Takahashi was very quiet, her face utterly drained of color, haggard and exhausted and lined with a sense of profound disappointment. It seemed clear in that moment that she understood, finally and irrefutably, that she would never discover what had happened to her son, that he had appeared briefly amidst that small chain of little towns that ran up and down the railroad, he had walked the orchard rows one last time for five weeks or six weeks or more, and then had winked out of her life and likely out of existence for reasons she would never know.

"Is there anywhere else you'd like to go?" I asked her as the Pontiac's hood flashed in the hot late afternoon sunlight.

"I'd like to go home now," she said simply.

"All right," I told her, and piloted the car back to my grandmother's, where Mrs. Takahashi slipped out immediately, muttering a quick, plain, "Thank you," and then closed the rear door.

Mrs. Wilson's voice beside me, its tone absent, lilting: "She still thinks her boy's some kind of hero."

"He fought in the 442nd," I said. "Doesn't that qualify?"

"No," she said firmly. "Don't you know that he came back here to ruin me? Can't you see that?"

"To ruin you? To ruin you? My God, he didn't even know what was happening."

"So why didn't he just leave? It's like he just couldn't let it go. He just had to keep hounding us all."

It was too much and I was angry now but before I could speak again, Mrs. Wilson said: "She had a boyfriend, you know. Not the man she married but they were serious. A local boy named Fisher."

"Helen? You mean Helen had a boyfriend?"

"Of course I mean Helen. That thing with Ray wasn't special. It was just a—just a—stupid—well, he seduced her is what it was. A sixteen-year-old girl. A child, really. God—he just wouldn't leave. I mean he did eventually, obviously, but—it was like having a big spider hiding in the house somewhere and you never knew which cup it'd be under."

"He just wanted a clear answer why you'd kicked his family out of their home. That's all."

"They were tenants, John," she said sternly. "I'm not required to give them any answer at all."

"They were more than tenants."

If she heard this she did not acknowledge it, instead talking over me, saying things now that she should have said a month or more before, even twenty-seven years before. "It was that thing at the diner that brought it to a head. After that she would hardly speak to me at all. So you see I had to do something, didn't I? As a mother, didn't I have to do something?"

"What do you mean? What are you saying?"

"Well," she said, and for a long time that was all. Then her voice started up again, resigned: "This is not to be repeated. Not to that woman or anyone else. Are we clear?"

I nodded and she looked out the window toward the street. I thought she would begin her story, whatever it was to be, but instead she nodded into the darkness and told me we would have to drive there.

11

ON THE DRIVE TO AUBURN, MRS. WILSON TOLD ME WHAT SHE
had, up to that point, kept in secret: that Ray had come to
her home—"My home!" she exclaimed, baffled and outraged
even years later—and that she had run him off the property.
She had thought that would be the end of it, but of course he
returned the next day. This time her husband was present.
He and the boy—a man now, a soldier who had been under
fire and had killed, done things that Homer Wilson had never
done and never would—had words there on the porch. Homer
tried at first to be reasonable, but Ray kept asking why why
why no matter what her husband said to him until Homer
lost his temper, a rare event, his fleshy freckled countenance
reddening from the end of his nose to the tips of his outsized
ears. "Get off my property or so help me God I'll have you
thrown in jail," his voice raised in a howl, indignant, bereft of
patience, and still harboring the secret knowledge that here

stood the father of his own grandson. He was unable to look him directly in the face, a face which must have reminded him of his friend Tak and all that had been before and all that would never be again. He had never seen the baby, neither of the men had, and although Mrs. Wilson did not say it I could not help but wonder if there was a great swath of loss running through Homer Wilson on that porch, that it had come to this, that in another world he might have embraced this boy as a son to replace the one that was lost.

The war was over now, of course, but those years in which the names of the dead appeared in the newspaper had hardly closed at all. The regular news conferred a kind of terrible celebrity, those families anointed by the war's great scythe becoming, through tragedy itself, the sudden center point and fulcrum of countless whispered conversations, as if giving full voice to those names—the names of the war dead—would somehow draw the attention of that dark reaper. Delivery of that news was—and this directly from Mrs. Wilson's lips—the purview of the postman, Eddie Farwell, a short, timid man of forty during the war years, whose unlucky lot was to deliver the Western Union telegrams announcing what amounted to a roll call of dead boys.

```
MR HOMER E WILSON
        NEWCASTLE CALIFORNIA

THE SECRETARY OF THE ARMY HAS ASKED ME
TO EXPRESS HIS DEEP REGRET THAT YOUR SON
PRIVATE FIRST CLASS JAMES WILSON DIED
FEBRUARY 21 IN PACIFIC AREA WHILE IN
```

PERFORMANCE OF HIS DUTIES AND SERVICE OF
HIS COUNTRY LETTER FOLLOWS

ULIO   THE ADJUTANT GENERAL

That quiet man in his rattling mail wagon seemed to shrink in the span of those years until he was nothing more than the gray ghost of his former self, one ghost carrying news from a whole world of ghosts.

Despite the fact that many of the residents of Placer County could draw their family trees to England and France and Italy and even Germany, few had been to any of those places, the dusty, sepia-toned photographs of their ancestors—our ancestors, since I am speaking, of course, of that dreaded but hardly universal *we* —providing a tenuous link. The great war machine in Europe boiled in us as if our homelands were overrun by the unwashed barbarian hordes of our nightmares, homelands we assumed were little different from our lives in Newcastle or Auburn or Loomis or any of the other little towns up and down the old highway, the European languages mostly forgotten, but the culture sharing a common root so when our boys died on that soil it was not so foreign as it might have been otherwise. It was Europe, after all; the people there looked like us and spoke languages we could at least recognize as languages. That was enough to bind us to a common sense of shared humanity.

But there was also, of course, the other war, the war in the Pacific, a landscape that felt different from us, separate from us, more savage, more *other*. The Midway Atoll, the long bloodbath of Guadalcanal, the Battles of Tenaru and the Eastern Solomons and Matanikau. And so Tarawa and Makin and Eniwetok. And so Saipan and Angaur and Iwo Jima and Okinawa. And so Hiroshima. And so Nagasaki. We did not feel the Japanese dead. We would have dropped a thousand atomic bombs on every one of their cities and we would have watched them become ash over and over because they had taken our children, our boys, and they would pay as long as there was yet breath in our lungs. Jimmy Wilson's end came on the island of Iwo Jima in the shadow of the great rock hulk of Mount Suribachi, a bullet passing through his chest so that he just had time to look down to the torn front of his uniform shirt where the blood was already pumping from the pressure of the final beat of his heart. He died facedown in the sand, and if he cursed his killers or thought of his bosom friend or of a girl or of his country or of anything at all, I do not know. What I know is that he died like so many others on some island he had never heard of and did not care about, fighting an enemy he did not know and could not understand. Seven thousand in February of 1945. Millions more in the years since. And millions more to come.

Mrs. Wilson and I reached what turned out to be a café, a quaint, box-like room on Auburn's main street, a roadway lined with old-fashioned businesses from a different time, redolent of nostalgia for an era that likely never existed at all. Memory filtered out the horrors so that what remained was that gauzy yellow light and the feeling that there had been, once upon a time, a period in which life was better than it would ever be again, the children respectful of their elders, the fruit heavy on the boughs, the rules just and easy to follow.

What the street stood for, at least for me, was something that had come up again and again whenever I spoke to anyone about 1945. They did not remember Ray Takahashi but what they did recall was an abiding sense of joy, for the war was over and the whole country was jubilant with success, with victory, especially in the small communities up and down what had been the old highway. There had been parades here in Auburn, likely on the very street where Mrs. Wilson had directed me drive her Pontiac, parades meant to celebrate the victors, spaced in ranks and led by open-topped cars filled with waving girls and square-jawed older men, their hair shorn to stubble as if in tribute to those discharged veterans.

"Are you hungry?" Mrs. Wilson said from the passenger seat. "Let me buy us dinner."

"Why are we here?"

"Let's go inside," she said. "I'm feeling peckish."

What I wanted more than anything was to shift the car into park, open its door, and simply walk away. I knew, I think, that what would come next would be the truth, and yet, perhaps strangely, I did not know that I wanted to hear it. I had already agreed not to tell Mrs. Takahashi, not even to tell my grandmother, and so were Mrs. Wilson to tell me the next piece of the story I would become complicit in her lie, in her secret. I already was.

But in the end I followed her into the quiet interior of the diner with its muted sounds of cutlery and its warm savory smell of grease and meat and potatoes, and I sat and listened to Mrs. Wilson, to her admission which was also tinged with the steadfast belief that she was, that she had been, in the right to do what she had done.

"She was eating with her beau," Mrs. Wilson told me.

"Helen was?"

"Yes, Helen," she said. "I don't know where in the restaurant but let's say it was right here at this table. I wasn't here, you understand. I was at home, but Helen told me all about it. You bet she did."

"I thought you said she wouldn't talk to you afterwards."

"No, that was a bit later, but I could tell it all came from that night. She was so upset, John. Just hysterical, really. It took me several hours to calm her down."

"What happened?" I asked her then. I had ordered a chicken-fried steak and the waitress set the thick white plate upon the table before me, asking us if there was anything else and then disappearing to other tables and other customers.

"Well, like I said," Mrs. Wilson told me then, "Helen was eating with her beau."

———

RAY TAKAHASHI HAD BEEN in Placer County for nearly six weeks when he stepped into that diner. He had been to the Wilsons' property four or five times in that period, although during all but the first two instances he had been held back at the property line, for Mr. Wilson had hired a group of local pickers (Mrs. Wilson, actually, although it had been Mr. Wilson who paid them) to stand at the road and ensure that he came no farther than the ditch. Undoubtedly they had called him all variety of slurs, racial and otherwise, but he never rose to whatever challenge they offered, holding back along the gravel of the roadway in his increasingly dusty uniform, hot and sweating in the lengthening summer sun. Perhaps he also came under the darkness of moonlight, skating in under the trees and watching the house, looking up at the windows for any trace of Jimmy or Helen, Jimmy's always dark but seeing light in Helen's and perhaps even her shape there. Perhaps too he wandered in that same darkness to the house in which he had spent all his life until the buses and the war—that small whitewashed house, in need of repairs and fresh paint now as it never had been when his own family had lived there. That house was filled with light and the shapes of its new residents, from Oklahoma and whose names he did not even know. Perhaps one of the men who had taunted him from the road was husband to the woman he had seen when he had first arrived and had stood in front of that house, for the men who guarded the Wilsons' driveway were not men whom Ray knew but were from elsewhere, in town only for the summer months, for the picking and processing, and then would scatter southward into fields of apples and grapefruit and oranges.

He would not have entered the diner had he not seen her through the front window, and for a long while he could only stand on the sidewalk, peering into the darkness, at first unbelieving and then realizing that yes it was her, it was Helen, at long last. There she was, seated across the room with a young man Ray did not know and hardly noticed at all.

"Helen," he said. He had already pulled the door open and stood squinting into the muted light of the interior, the room quieting as diners turned to look, their forks suspended in the air, his shape in the doorway rigid, uniformed. Then the waitress was beside him, her voice hovering somewhere between whisper and wail: "I'm sorry but you can't be in here. We just can't serve you. I'm sorry but it's just our policy," and his response was baffled surprise, not even understanding until that moment what kind of room, what kind of business, he had stepped into. "What? What?" focused all the while on Helen, his eyes still adjusting to the muted light. He felt himself pulled toward her even as the waitress continued to speak, "You can't be in here, it's not for you, didn't you see the sign?" and him continuing to mumble, "What? What?" even as he pushed past her.

When he reached Helen's table, the waitress was still there like some insect fluttering around his face, repeating something so that Helen had to look from Ray to the waitress and then to her dining companion who had stood now and was also talking, "Can I help you, bud? What's the trouble here?" his voice amicable, his hand on Ray's arm as if to reassure him that everything would be fine.

"Helen," he said.

And her voice, when it came, was like an exhale: "Oh Ray."

"I've been trying—"

But the waitress now, again: "You're gonna have to leave. We don't serve you people here. We just don't. It's policy."

"I just need to speak to—"

"You've gotta go right out that door or I'm calling the police."

"Ma'am, if you'll just—"

"Right out that door. I'm calling the police. They'll—"

"Go ahead! Go ahead and call them. Call whoever you want." And when the waitress did not move he shouted at her again: "Well, go on then. Make your phone call."

"Whoa bud," the man at his elbow said. Ray looked at him now. A plain-faced young man barely out of his teens, white of course, skin tanned from a summer of sunlight, his shirt clean denim, dressed, Ray thought, not unlike how he might have dressed in those days before. He turned to see the look on Helen's face, her sense of confusion, guilt, fear, horror at seeing him there.

"Will you talk to me?" And when she did not respond he said her name.

"Look, bud," the man said, "maybe you and I should head outside."

"Helen," Ray said again.

"You've got to go, Ray," she said then, quietly, not looking at him now, her eyes averted. "Just leave. Just leave us alone."

"Please," he said.

Mrs. Wilson told me that the young man at the table was Helen's beau, Ed Fisher, and that he and Helen had been dating for three months, although the night Ray happened upon her at the diner would be their last date, their connection dissipating all at once like water into sand. But now he was there at Ray's side, wiry and muscular, not slack but not a soldier either, or at least not a veteran of combat, and a head taller than Ray. When he spoke again his voice was firm and resolute and direct: "I'm gonna ask you to step away from our table, bud."

The waitress had disappeared now, perhaps to call the police, the diner around them utterly frozen as if in tableau.

"I've been to the house," Ray said.

"I know."

"They told you?"

"Yes."

"I've been trying to see you. To talk to you."

"Ray, this is my boyfriend. Ed Fisher. Ed—this is Ray. My . . . well, he used to be my neighbor."

"Your neighbor?" Ray said.

"Now you should go," she said. "You don't live here any-more, Ray."

And then another question, one which had been eating at him for all those weeks and which he might have asked anyone he had come across, even the priest at the Buddhist church, but had not because, in his heart, he already knew the answer: "Where's Jimmy, Helen?"

"Jimmy?"

"Where is he? Is he still in the army?"

"Ray," Helen said quietly. Just that.

She did not have to say more. The force of it was unexpected: a hard blow that seemed to strike him everywhere at once as if the air itself had solidified around him and then pressed in so that the whole of him—not just his body but everything he was—seemed all at once to crush in on itself.

"Ah no," he said. "Goddammit. Goddammit."

"Come on, bud," Fisher said at his arm, and while a moment before Ray might well have swung on him, on his bland tan face, might have swung on him and might have kept on swing-ing in rage and terror and despair, now he let that thin hard grip turn him away from the table, glancing back at Helen one final time, her face a mask of confusion and concern and even sadness. But not love. And Ray hoped he would never see that face again.

———

WE WERE SILENT THEN. Looking down at my empty plate with its smears of grease, I thought inexplicably of Chiggers and our talk at that Denny's across town and how we managed, all into that smoky night, to skip over the real topic of our conversation, the one neither of us would bring up except in the thinnest and most fleeting of terms. He had not called me on the way back home to San Diego and I was thankful for that even as a deep pang of regret thumped my ribs.

"You think I was wrong?"

I looked up at her. "I'm sure you did what you thought best."

"Thank you, John," she said.

She looked away now, her eyes out past me toward the window that faced the street, eyes so startlingly blue that they appeared as if chips of ice.

"What happened next?" I said.

"Next?"

"In the car you said that you had to do something after Helen saw him here. So what was it? What did you do?"

"I didn't do anything any mother wouldn't have done."

"What did you do?"

In the muted light of the diner I could almost see the woman she had been at thirty or twenty or even the girl she had been before that, the years stripped away and the ghost of her former self just beyond the light of those years, when the future had been yet open and the stakes controlled by choices never as dire as those to come after.

"Well, I'll tell you what I did," she said at last, her spine seeming to straighten at the words, her neck and head elevating. "I did what my daughter asked me to do. And she was right to ask me. I had my husband pay some of the men to chase him off. He left me no choice."

"Who did it?"

"Just some men who worked for us on the property. Migrants.

They left at the end of the picking. What does it matter who they were?"

"What happened?"

"Well, he left, didn't he?"

"Jesus Christ."

"You'll have children of your own one day. Then you'll understand. You'd do anything for your children. Anything."

For all the years that followed that evening I have wished that I would have said something of value in that moment, something which might have served to lay bare all the truths and lies we had been snaking through during the blazing heat of that summer, something that would make sense of it, or even something more banal, a curse of anger or of despair, a damnation leveled at this woman whose deceit had blown apart not only her own family but Ray Takahashi's family as well. But no words came, and in the end I only sat there, staring down at my empty dinner plate, my sweating water glass.

"She was so young. And I didn't know what she'd do if she saw him again. I was afraid she'd fall right back into his arms. I don't expect you to understand but I thought Helen would, maybe not at first but certainly after she had her own children. I thought she'd understand then at least."

"Do you regret it?"

"Had you asked me that a few months ago I might have said no. Now I'm just not sure. It's a strange feeling to have no family. I don't even know where my daughter lives anymore. Last time I wrote her the letter was returned. Not at this address. Phone disconnected or changed. No forwarding number. Not in the phone book. It's like she just disappeared."

"Like Ray," I said.

And now she looked at me and the expression that passed over her face was like a thousand clouds at once. The youth I had seen before was gone now and in its place stood every moment of her sixty-nine years, a woman who was, I realized, broken by all the decisions she had ever made.

"Come on," I told her. "It's getting late."

"John."

"It's all right," I said.

FOR THE REST OF THAT SUMMER I returned to the relative mundanity of my days before Mrs. Wilson and Mrs. Takahashi had entered my life. I thought often of calling Ray's mother to tell her what I had learned, but each time something held me back, not a sense of loyalty to family or to race but perhaps simply the knowledge that what I had learned did not amount to much at all. He had been run off the property and did not return. Still, I wondered why Mrs. Wilson had chosen to tell me, to tell anyone at all, since she had very nearly gotten through Mrs. Takahashi's visits without any of it being known. And really what did it matter now that she had told me? Was it such a great secret in the end? After all of it, no one really knew what happened to Raymond Takahashi and yet Mrs. Wilson had even kept what little she had known a secret, allowing the boy's mother to make the drive not once or twice but six times in all, allowing her to trace the ghosts of a history that was obfuscated by Mrs. Wilson herself. Help me, Evelyn, Mrs. Takahashi had said. Perhaps it was simply loneliness, that she might have clung to Mrs. Takahashi in the emptiness of her final decades, their lives inexplicably re-entwined amidst the ghosts of a past the repercussions of which continued to reverberate well into whatever future was yet to come.

And so I returned to my work at the gas station, and when classes started at the nearby community college I spoke to a counselor and signed up for a general education course in math and another in creative writing. I sat uncomfortably at the back of the room, listening to the professors drone on and watching the door.

In the evenings I would sit out on the back porch, smoking and staring at the still-unkempt patch of lawn and the twisted black shape of the wild plum, a survivor, I imagined, from some orchard that might well have been tended and cared for in the days before the war. It was there, in the shortening days of late September, when I began to wonder about my friend Chiggers again. Perhaps I thought to call him because I now knew more of the story I had begun to tell him on the same porch when the summer was young and the days moved toward their own vigor. It was not my story, it never had been, and even so, my part in it was over. Ray Takahashi would forever be lost amidst the golden grasses and blue oaks and cold clear streams.

Chiggers had written his phone number on a scrap of paper and I had come across it a few days earlier next to my typewriter, an artifact which was finally getting some use once more now that I was in school. One cool cloudy night in early fall, after my grandmother had stuck her head outside to tell me that she was going to bed, I determined it was time for me to contact my old friend. I waited outside until I thought my grandmother likely asleep, then I stubbed out my cigarette and reentered the darkening interior of the house, dialing those scrawled digits and then leaning against the wall as that distant telephone in San Diego began to ring.

The woman who answered sounded, even in her one-word greeting, exhausted and I worried for a moment that I had called too late at night. I did not even know what time it was. Surely not far past eight. "Uh, hello," I mumbled in response to her voice. "This is . . . uh . . . this is John Frazier. I'm a friend of Chiggers'."

"Who?" the woman said.

"Chig—" I began, stopped, said, "Shoot," and then realized with a start that I could not remember his real name. "I'm his friend from Victnam. I'm sorry, we called him Chiggers. My name's John. He called me Flip."

"Oh Flip, sí," she said. And then the name: "Hector."

"Hector, right right," I said. "This is his mother?"

"Claro que sí."

"I'm sorry to call so late."

"Not so late."

I thought she would tell me to wait then, that she would go find Chiggers or that he was out, but she lapsed into silence again and so I said, finally, "Is he around? Can I speak with him?"

"Oh no, not around."

"Will he be back soon?"

"No. Se murió."

I could feel, in that moment, a fierce wild descent, as if I had slipped from some high precipice and was now flailing toward the distant earth, the helicopter blades chopping the air above me, the sawgrass racing up in its vast endless plain. "He's dead?"

"Walked into the sea." There was an edge of emotion in her voice but she did not break down, did not fall into weeping.

"He drowned?"

"He was a good boy," she said. And then, without saying goodbye, there was the faintest click and the phone was silent.

The sound I made was something like a bark or a cry, a sort of explosion that welled up out of my heart like black bile. That morning, I had sat at this very table and had eaten a piece of toast with strawberry jam and drained a cup of Maxwell House with milk from my grandmother's refrigerator, and all that time Chiggers was dead. When I thought of him then and when I was to think of him in all the years to come and when I think of him now it is of a forest of black pines and a cold, hard surf rolling in upon a gray beach. And Chiggers, tiny against that great sweep of mist, stepping forward into the sea, fully clothed, his body as black as those trees, as gray as the surf, as dark as the sky.

It could happen, I knew, to anyone. The sniper's sight still tracked my shape through the palms, the bamboo, through the wild plum in the backyard, and here, at the kitchen table.

My grandmother stood in the doorway to her bedroom, her nightgown held tight around her shapeless body. "John?" she called to me, her voice coming as if from across some great and terrible distance. "Are you all right? John?"

"No," I said, my body seeming to come all apart as the first of the waves tumbled in from the wine-dark sea. "I'm not all right. I'm not all right. I'm not."

12

I CANNOT FIND ALL OF THE DAYS IMMEDIATELY AFTER speaking to Chiggers's mother, but one of the great horrors of heroin is that there is no merciful blackout attached to its sharp vinegar scent, which is to say that I remember more than I care to admit. Picture what you would like and I will tell you that it was probably worse: a lost weekend cliché of strippers and dope and alcohol and all the rest. When I found myself at last it was upon a stinking, seaweed-covered beach in a twilight that I realized eventually was not dusk but dawn, my body reeking of alcohol and seawater. What day it was I did not yet know, nor the location of the beach upon which I lay chattering with cold. Out beyond the edge of the shushing breakers ran a wall of end-less fog that wrapped the whole of that landscape in a blurred and gauzy half-light. My pockets were empty, not only of cash but of my wallet and of any and all forms of identification. For a long while I simply lay there in the sand, feeling the sick-ness of life itself as it washed over me, staring out across the

Pacific in the direction of Asia, of Vietnam, and, it occurred to me somewhat later, of Japan, and in the direction in which my friend Chiggers had walked into the sea, as if in doing so he might cross that gray ocean to return to the place where everything had gone so terribly wrong.

When at last I tried to rise, the movement came with a paroxysm of vomiting that staggered me back to the sand for several agonizing minutes until what ran from my chapped lips was only bile and thin spittle and finally nothing at all. What I knew, what I thought of, was that if I could take just two hits, two quick puffs from the foil, inhale no more than a lungful, a half lungful, all this sickness would go away in an instant and I would be well again. God help me but sometimes I still think this even all these years later. That I was able to clamber achingly to my feet was a kind of miracle and then to stumble away from the water was yet another, weaving up the high winded crests of the dunes and mercifully away from the bracingly cold wind that ran in a wet gusty stream off the gray face of that sea of fog. Were it not for the chill of the fog I might well have wondered if I had fallen into my own memory of Vietnam and, even though I knew it impossible, had I come upon a thick band of jungle palms atop the shelter of the dunes I would have been terrified but not surprised.

And yet when I came away from that oceanic dunescape it was into a sleepy San Francisco neighborhood, a fact I confirmed by inquiring of a passing bicyclist, a woolen-clad long-haired and beaded hippie of a type I had seen in *Life* magazine but rarely outside those pages, certainly not in my parents' Alhambra. "San Fran, my man," he said when I asked where I was, and then he was gone, flitting out in a slow undulating loop spun broadside to the sea's wind.

I found my grandmother's car soon after stumbling out of the dunes, either by luck or providence or from some dim remembrance of where I had parked it, neatly and inconspicuously at the curb just a few dozen meters away. The vehicle was unmolested and apparently undamaged, the keys yet there on the floor just under the driver's seat, where my grandmother was in the habit of keeping them and where I, even in my alcohol- and drug-induced haze, had apparently left them in turn. I must have passed out again there in the car, for I awoke a few hours later, hungry and thirsty beyond all reason, the sky the color of dead flesh and a faint perspiration of greasy rain hovering in the air. A search confirmed what I already suspected would be true, that my wallet was nowhere to be found in the vehicle, and so, without money or identification of any kind, I concluded that I had little choice but to drive back to Newcastle, a decision almost immediately rendered impossible when I turned on the ignition and realized that the vehicle's fuel gauge was nearly touching the *E*. I could hardly get to Berkeley, let alone all the way across the Sacramento Valley and up into the foothills of Placer County.

I sat there weighing my options and feeling the heavy tide of guilt and shame wash over me, but at last I walked to a pay phone and called my grandmother collect, hoping that she would pick up but also that she would not.

"Gran?" I said, my voice croaking. "It's John."

"Oh honey," she said, "you scared the hell out of me. Are you all right?"

"I'm fine."

"You're in big trouble, boy-o," she said. "You scared an old lady half to death."

"I know I did. I'm sorry, Gran. I don't even know . . ." I trailed off then. What more could I say? There was nothing I could tell her.

"Where are you?"

"San Francisco," I said.

"Not so far," she said. "You can be home in a few hours."

"I don't have any money," I said. "My wallet's gone. I guess it got stolen."

"Well, we can deal with that when you get here."

"There's not enough gas to get that far," I said. "I can maybe get halfway. Maybe as far as Vallejo." Then I shook my head. "I don't know what to do." I lay my forehead against the cool metal panel of the pay phone's booth.

She was silent for a moment. "I've got half a mind to make you walk home," she said then. She waited, as if I might offer to do just that, and when I said nothing in response she told me to read her the number of the pay phone, which I did, and then told me to hang up and wait there for her call.

In the hours of my exhausted slumber in the front seat of the car, the city had come fully awake, traffic on the wide span of the street slipping by in waves. I wondered if I could find the bar at which I had, two or three nights before, bought a small sticky lump of black tar heroin and if I could somehow talk that same dealer into giving me just a tiny bit more on credit. Perhaps the dealer would buy the car, or perhaps we might make a trade. I wanted to die.

When the phone rang I jumped up from the curb, surprised and shocked at the loudness of that sound. "Hello, hello?" I croaked into the handset.

"John?"

"Yes, it's me."

"Do you have enough gasoline to get to my house?"

It took a moment for me to understand that although the voice was a woman's, it was not the voice of my grandmother. "Who is this?" I asked.

"Kimiko Takahashi," she said.

"Mrs. Takahashi?"

"Do you remember how to get here?"

"Yes."

"You come here, John."

My eyes were overbrimming with tears now. "I'm sick," I said.

"Then I'll come get you. Tell me where you are."

"No, no," I said. "Jesus." I sniffled, trying in vain to master myself, feeling instead just how tired I was, just how utterly and completely exhausted. "I can get there. I can make it that far, I think."

"I'll be waiting here for you. Come straight here. You hear me, John? Come straight to my house."

"All right," I said.

And that was exactly what I did.

———

I HAD HOPED, on the drive to San Jose, that Mrs. Takahashi would simply hand me a few dollars by which I could gas up my grandmother's sedan and make the drive back to Newcastle, but when I arrived it was to find her waiting for me on her porch, hands on hips, appraising my condition as I stepped achingly out of the car. "Come inside," she said.

"I'm filthy," I told her.

"You come inside now," she said, her voice so stern that I almost expected her to stamp her foot like a mother scolding a recalcitrant child.

I did as she bade me, removing my shoes before entering the house and then marching into the bathroom. "Soap." She pointed. "Shampoo. Leave your clothes here. I'll wash."

"You don't have to do that," I mumbled, but she only shook her head.

"I'll get you a robe to wear."

I can hardly explain how grateful I was but also how ashamed. When I emerged at last it was wearing the thick terry-cloth bathrobe I had found hanging from the inside of the door. The smell that came from the kitchen was savory and thick. Mrs. Takahashi entered the room in the same moment, pointing to the little kitchen table at which I had, months before, in the first blush of that now-gone summer, listened to Mrs. Wilson stammer out her questions about the whereabouts of Mrs. Takahashi's son and at which I now sat as Mrs. Takahashi went to the stove and opened it and brought out a baking dish and a moment later delivered a steaming hot plate of chicken enchiladas, their curves bubbling with cheese, rice and refried beans on the side.

"You eat," she said simply. "You'll feel better then."

"I'm sorry," I said through my tears. "Thank you so much."

"John," she said.

I paused mid-bite to look at her, her dark eyes staring back at my own, fixing me in their gaze.

"You'll be okay," she said. "You will."

I mumbled something in the affirmative.

After a time she nodded. "I'm going to check the laundry," she said. "There's more in the pan on the stove."

"It's so good," I said, smiling now, smiling and crying, a kind of delirium possessing me so that I did not know if I was ecstatic or on the verge of death itself.

"My husband," she said. "He's obsessed with Mexican food. It's all we ever eat anymore."

———

I CLEANED THAT PLATE and refilled it and cleaned it again until the enchilada pan was empty. When I was done I sat back in the kitchen chair, my hands in my lap, the only sounds those of the road outside somewhere beyond the shaded window and the ticking of a clock.

I do not know how many people I am responsible for killing in Vietnam, which is a clever way of saying I do not know how many people I killed. I had been in the country for a year as part of an invading army and the only Vietnamese person I could recall with any detail was a Saigon prostitute I—and Chiggers—called by her working name: Daisy. And yet I had killed and killed and killed and each of them had mothers and fathers and grandparents and some had been children and all had been loved and named and loved again. And I radioed and the Phantoms came and they brought napalm and white phosphorus and Sidewinders and Zunis and all the rest and those people, loved and named, became pillars of ash washed away by the monsoon rain.

When Mrs. Takahashi finally appeared she held a folded sheet of paper in one hand and she set it upon the sideboard before crossing her arms and nodding briefly. "I have more," she said. "My husband likes tamales too. There are some in the freezer."

"I'm stuffed," I said. "Thank you."

"Good tamales," she said. "At least he thinks so."

"He's really gone nuts for Mexican?"

"Every day," she said. "It's all he'll eat now. If I make anything else he complains."

"You make them from scratch?"

"Not the tamales. They come from a market across town. He's picky."

"Is he?"

"About the tamales. Not so much about anything else."

There was, between us, a moment of silence then, the afternoon's gray rain spattering the house, but within there were no sounds but those of the room itself, our breath on the air, the ticking of the clock. "I'm sorry," I said to her.

"You don't need to be sorry," she said. "You needed help. And we're friends."

"I'm a bad person."

"Why?"

I shook my head. "I don't even know where to start. You know I was in Vietnam."

"That was war, John."

"No," I said roughly. "I mean yes, but no."

"You have to forgive yourself."

"How?"

"It's past," she said simply.

"But what am I supposed to do?"

She looked at me. "You're supposed to live," she said. "That's all. Just live."

Mrs. Takahashi lifted the sheet of paper from the sideboard and slid it before me on the kitchen table. I asked her what it was before I even looked at it but she did not answer, not at first, allowing me a moment to take in what was, I realized, a copy of a telegram.

"Would you take this to Mrs. Wilson for me?" Mrs. Takahashi said after a time. "I had them make an extra copy. I was going to mail it to her."

"What is it?"

"It's him. Franklin R. Yamada," she said.

"Who?" But even in saying this single syllable I understood who she meant.

"My grandson," she said, and in response my voice emitted a sound that was part exhale and part moan.

```
MR AND MRS ROBERT F YAMADA,
DONT PHONE DONT DELIVER BETWEEN
10PM AND 6AM REPORT DELIVERY

8722 WILLIAMS DR SEATTLE WA

THE SECRETARY OF THE ARMY HAS ASKED ME TO
EXPRESS HIS DEEP REGRET THAT YOUR SON, RIFLE-
MAN FRANKLIN R. YAMADA DIED IN VIETNAM ON 28
MARCH 1968, FROM WOUND RECEIVED WHILE ON COM-
BAT OPERATION.
```

PLEASE ACCEPT MY DEEPEST SYMPATHY. THIS CON-
FIRMS PERSONAL NOTICIATION MADE BY A REPRE-
SENTATIVE OF THE SECRETARY OF THE ARMY

KENNETH G WICKHAM MAJOR GENERAL USA F59 THE
ADJUTANT GENERAL (17).

"He died in Vietnam?"

"Yes," she said.

"God not even . . . a year?—year and a half?"

"Yes."

"Are you sure this is him? Couldn't it be a mistake?"

"This is him, John," she said. "My grandson's name was Franklin. Sounds funny to me. Franklin. I don't think Ray would have named him that. Do you?" Her tone was plain but there was, I thought, an edge somewhere beneath.

"How did you find him?"

"My husband called his lawyer friend and his lawyer friend called a private investigator. He tracked it down from what Evelyn left."

"She left something?" But then I remembered that day when she had placed that single sheet of paper upon the coffee table in the living room, when she had said that this was all she knew.

"The birth certificate," Mrs. Takahashi said. "So we knew the date and location and they figured out the rest. I don't know how. It doesn't really matter anymore."

"Yamada," I said. "That's a Japanese name?"

She did not say anything now, only staring down at the little sheet of paper on the tabletop.

"God, Mrs. Takahashi," I said then. "There's something I need to tell you," for the thought of it, that I harbored this last piece of information, the piece that my aunt had told me and for which she had sworn me to secrecy, that piece I could hold in secret no longer and so I told her, in one long gasping monologue, about that moment in the diner in Auburn and about how Evelyn Wilson—at Helen's behest—had hired some fruit pickers to chase Ray out of the county, how Mrs. Wilson had been, all those weeks, not an ally at all but a kind of enemy.

Mrs. Takahashi raised her palm. "I already know," she said.

I sat staring at her, goggle-eyed. "But how? She told me no one else knew."

"I knew she wasn't telling me the truth," Mrs. Takahashi said. "Or not all of it. So I came back three or four times and asked around myself. I found someone who worked for her back then, when he was a boy. Bishop was his name. He remembered my Raymond in his uniform. He—he liked him. He told me my son was a hero."

"My God, Mrs. Takahashi. He was. He was a hero. Jesus." The tears were coming again but I had been washed dry of them now and the sobs were empty.

In the end it had been so simple: a lawyer and a private detective and here was the telegram after just a few months. I had not been needed at all and my aunt had only obfuscated and slowed down the process. The Takahashis only needed us to get out of the way. It was their own story, not mine and not even my aunt's, but of course that had always been true. And what I thought in that moment was that had the clock just rolled back two years or three or four or ten or God all the way back to the start, had Mrs. Takahashi just known or had Evelyn Wilson had the courage, they might have found him in time, before the army had taken him and Vietnam had blown the ghost from his skin. Our tours had overlapped, so it was even possible that I had seen him in the endless mud field of that base on the Nine Dragon River. In my shivering horror of that possibility, I stand below the Huey that will deliver him to his death, the insectoid shape hovering in the flat white light, its blades chopping the air. That moment seems to last forever but finally the machine drifts away, turning in a lazy arc out across the wire and into the jungle. It is almost beautiful, like a leaf upon the wind.

"I wish I could have known him," I said.

"He would have liked you," Mrs. Takahashi told me, and I nearly asked her how she could know such a thing but then I understood that she was not talking about her grandson Franklin Yamada but about Ray, Raymond, her son.

"I hope you're right," I said simply.

"I'm his mother," she said. "Of course I'm right."

13

IF THIS STORY HAD ENDED THERE I DO NOT KNOW IF I EVER would have written it down. The heat of that summer and the chill of winter passed until spring came again and another summer. I had moved back to Southern California by that time, having failed out of community college in Placer County, so that when I registered at Pasadena City College it was to start completely over. In most ways I did not mind. There are few moments in our lives when we are allowed to begin anew.

It was from Pasadena that I mailed my aunt the sheet of paper that Mrs. Takahashi had given me the autumn before. I had held on to it out of cowardice, for I did not want to see her and so would not drive to her home to deliver the document in person and hesitated in mailing it when I was yet in Placer County for fear she would come visit me to discuss its particulars. I am quite sure she wondered why I had mailed it to her from Southern California, for it might have implied that Mrs. Takahashi and I were still in touch, which we were

not, our lives untethered from each other's in the same way my
life had become untethered from Mrs. Wilson's. We had told a
story together, in a way, and that story was over now and there
was nothing left between us but guilt and disappointment and
sadness. We did not find out what had really happened to Ray
Takahashi and at that point I assumed that we never would.
But in truth, it was only Mrs. Wilson and Mrs. Takahashi who
would never find out that last piece of information; it would, in
the end, be mine to bear alone.

Hiroshi Takahashi passed away just a year after I left Placer
County, in 1971. He was seventy years old and died in the grocery in San Jose where he had worked all those years after
returning from the camps. I never met him, not a single time,
and yet I felt I knew him somehow and drove up from Pasadena
for the funeral, picking up my grandmother on the way. She and
Mrs. Takahashi had kept in touch some, exchanging holiday
cards, and so it was my grandmother who had informed me of
Mr. Takahashi's passing. It had not been particularly long since
I had last seen Mrs. Takahashi, of course, only two years, and
yet under these circumstances it felt as if I had not seen her in a
good long while. I realized soon after pulling into the parking
lot that I was actually anxious at the idea of seeing her again.
The last time I had been quite literally a wreck, and while I
had managed to keep sober in the gap between our meetings,
I remained ashamed and mortified that she might think of me
in terms of that day when I wept and wept at her kitchen table
as she fed me reheated enchiladas, a meal intended for her husband's pleasure. That I did not meet him, I realized, was yet
another disappointment in a life that already seemed, at age
twenty-three, filled to the brim with them. That she greeted

me like an old friend, like a nephew she loved and had not seen in too many days, gave my heart a mighty lurch. She ran her fingers through my hair, told me I needed a haircut, and gently prodded my stomach. "Are you eating enough?" she asked me. "Do I need to bring you some enchiladas?"

My grandmother passed away three years later, quietly, in her bed in that house in Newcastle. My mother and her sisters fought over her will and the house was quickly sold and what profit there might have been disappeared between them. My first novel was out by then and Gran had at least seen a copy of it before her death. Only after she was gone did I understand that she had been the most important person in my life; she had been there by my side during the worst of the implosion of my soul, had summoned me back from San Francisco and had ministered to me and taken care of me and continued to call me every few weeks all through the years to follow. That those calls would no longer come felt a blow to my heart but one which, at least, felt natural and reasonable. She had been eighty-five years old and that seemed enough. I could not imagine myself living half that long, although now, not quite at the midpoint, I have a better imagination for the future.

Mrs. Takahashi's death in 1981 brought me to San Jose once more. My wife had put her on our Christmas card list—my wife was attuned to such things—and this had put us in some regular contact, enough so that one of her daughters had sent us the notice of her passing. After the funeral, I visited Mary and Doris, the two grown Takahashi daughters, although neither of their last names were Takahashi then and had not been for many years. I told them some about the summer of 1969 when their mother and my aunt had traversed the county looking for clues as to their elder brother's disappearance. He would have been—should have been—fifty-eight years old on the year of his mother's death and part of me still wondered if he was out there somewhere, walking the hills of some other land, resting under the shadows of some other trees. Mary told me of seeing Ray and Helen kissing on the day the buses came, their young bodies clasped to each other under the shade of the fruit sheds. "He had a little something from her," Doris remembered.

"What do you mean?"

"A little locket or something. He used to fidget with it all the time when he thought we weren't looking."

"He thought we were two blind little kids," Mary said.

"But we knew everything, didn't we?" Doris said, smiling.

"We sure did," Mary said.

But not everything, I thought.

———

AS FOR EVELYN WILSON, I did not hear much from her in the years that followed the end of this narrative. She never met my wife nor my children, although I did discover after her death that she had every one of my novels and clippings of some of my stories and essays too. I thought that she might well have been keeping track of my writing just to make sure she did not appear in those public pages. Until the appearance of this book, she would have been quite satisfied.

News of Mrs. Wilson's passing came during a phone call from my mother not so very long after Mrs. Takahashi's funeral. Just after her greeting, my mother asked if I remembered Evelyn Wilson "up there near Auburn," and I already knew what was coming. My grandmother's death had felt like a physical blow, and Mrs. Takahashi's had not been particularly different, but Mrs. Wilson's, much to my surprise, was the worst of all, and a hard heaviness flooded over me at the news. My daughter, six years old then, found me sitting on the kitchen floor near the phone, my head in my hands. "Daddy," she said, "are you hurt? Do you need a Band-Aid?"

"I'm all right, babydoll," I told her, but she climbed into my lap nonetheless and held my head in her tiny hands and rocked me and told me everything would be all right, as I had said to her dozens of times before.

I went there for the funeral, my first time in Newcastle since 1971, and stood around as people I did not know talked about her, and when a woman nearing sixty approached me after the service and asked if I was John Frazier, it took me a moment to place the name that she gave me in response. It was Helen, the daughter who had become so estranged from her mother that in 1969 they had not been in communication at all. She looked not unlike her mother had those years before, perhaps heavier but otherwise it would not have been difficult to identify her and I marveled at my own inability to do so. In the years that had followed I had not thought much of Helen Wilson, the daughter, the mother who had also lost her child, and I longed to ask her if she had reconciled with her own mother in the end and if she had learned what had become of her son, Franklin Yamada, but after handing me a business card she turned and walked away, the look on her face an inscrutable mask. I had seen just that expression from her mother and knew it would be foolish to press her.

"She seems pleasant," my wife said next to me.

"She just buried her mother," I told her.

"Oh jeez," my wife said. "I didn't know that was the daughter. You might have introduced us."

"I didn't know her," I said. "I've never seen her before."

"What's the card?"

I handed it to her and she read it aloud, the name of a law office in Auburn, and although I did not know or understand what it might have meant, my wife, smarter than I am in almost every way, said, "She left you something."

"What do you mean?"

"In her will. She left you something."

"No way," I said.

"I'll bet you a million dollars," my wife said.

———

MY WIFE, OF COURSE, WAS RIGHT. Stepping up to the lawyer's office I thought I would receive some kind of document of confession, that somehow Evelyn Wilson might have known the whole story of Ray Takahashi's disappearance and would only now, finally, reveal it to me, the last survivor of those days in which we searched for his whereabouts to no avail. But I was not handed any cryptic sealed envelope but instead was instructed to sit in the lawyer's unkempt office and was read the pertinent part of the last will and testament of Evelyn Florence Wilson. When the lawyer was done he looked up at me.

"I don't understand," I told him.

"What's not to understand?"

"What about her daughter? Her grandchildren?"

"It's yours, Mr. Frazier," he said. "Anyway, I don't think the daughter wants anything to do with it at all."

I shook my head. It did not seem possible but the lawyer assured me that it was true. I signed the documents and was instructed to visit the title company to complete the transfer. I did so with my wife and daughter present, after which the house and property atop the ridge, the old white Victorian in which the Wilson family had made their home and the twenty remaining acres that surrounded it, was officially transferred into my name.

———

AND SO IT IS HERE, in the late spring of 1983, that this story reaches its end. I have come to see what needs be done to the house and property, for my wife and I have decided to keep it, at least for now, and to use it as a summer getaway, a place in the country we can retire to when I am not teaching, to offer our daughter some version of those same childhood memories that I still hold dear. That my wife is pregnant again is another reason to hold the place in trust, for we are growing weary of the city. It could be that we move here permanently one day. This I do not yet know.

I have come to clean and repair and generally ready the house for the arrival of my wife and daughter and the baby yet to come, which really means that I have come here to write in this space while the contractor I have hired does what work needs doing: new siding to replace that which has rotted away, new roofing, new porch boards and a new rail, new steps off the back door. The original furniture remains in place, every stick of it, and I have taken some time here to go through the Wilsons' papers—old receipts and the like, ephemera of the days in which this house held a business and a family all at once. At some point I will take the important papers to the county office in Auburn to see if some archivist there can make use of them. I do not think I will throw them out if the county can find no purpose in the documents, for there are photographs and maps and business papers going back before the turn of the century and they provide a history of this place, one that I cannot bear to see destroyed. In that stack of papers is a photograph of a young Japanese man next to a white farmer. It is unlabeled but I can only assume that I am looking at Homer Wilson and Hiro Takahashi, their faces bright in the sun of some summer long past.

I have hired some landscapers to clear out the brush and trim the fruit trees that yet remain, remnants of that old orchard still somehow clinging to life. I have been told that the other house, the little house in which the Takahashis once lived, is no longer salvageable and that it should be torn down but have asked the laborers instead to block off the doors and windows so that my daughter will have no way of entering, for I cannot fathom removing that structure from the world. It feels, indeed, that I have no right to do so. I can see its sagging roofline from the upstairs bedroom, the one that I think must have been Helen's those many years ago, as I have found a series of girlish hearts inked upon the bottom of the windowsill where the bed was once pushed against the wall. From here the trees appear a second surface of the earth, one which could be walked across, soft and yielding but firm enough to hold my steps: oaks and loose fruit trees of what variety I do not yet know, their shapes like green clouds brought low from the sky to huddle close to the heat of the earth.

———

THE END OF THIS STORY arrived in mid-May, both unbidden and unexpected, its coming announced by the sound of a car crunching the gravel outside. My assumption was that another worker or laborer or contractor had arrived or departed, since that had been the steady traffic of the preceding three weeks, and so I was fully prepared to ignore that sound when a knock came on the screen.

What I found upon what I still thought of as Mrs. Wilson's porch was a somewhat portly man in a white shirt, perhaps fifty or so, his thinning hair slicked back from his head like some Southern revival preacher out of a Flannery O'Connor story. He told me his name was Jim Tuttle and asked if I was related to Mrs. Evelyn Wilson or the Wilson family. When I told him I was, he asked me in what way.

"Who are you?" I said. He said his name again and I shook my head. "What's this about?"

"Uh . . . well . . . ," he began, his balding pate already beaded with sweat. "It's about . . . well . . . I need to tell someone something."

"Tell what?"

"Are you Mrs. Wilson's son or . . . ?"

"She was my aunt," I said then, increasingly exasperated by this interruption and by the apparent reticence of this man Tuttle to explain his presence on my porch.

"Oh, your aunt," he said.

"What's this about?" I asked him again. "I'm right in the middle of something."

"Oh, I'm sorry," he said. "I would've called, but I didn't have the number."

"Called for what?"

"To arrange a time of more . . . uh . . . convenience."

"But to do what? Convenience for what?"

"Oh . . . of course . . . ," he said now, his face clouding with obvious concern and difficulty and distress. "You have no idea why I'm here."

"At this point, I'm not even sure *you* have any idea why you're here."

"Funny," he said without mirth. He was wearing a linen sport coat but it might as well have been wool for all the sweat his body was producing. "I came here to tell someone what happened," he said.

"To whom?"

"To my father."

"Who's your father?"

"Ed Tuttle Junior," he said.

"I don't think I can help you," I said. "I don't know anyone by that name. I think you've just gotten the wrong house."

"No, no," he said quickly, for I had half turned toward the interior again, toward my typewriter and its stack of pages. "It has to do with Mrs. Wilson. I just have to come clean is all. It's something that's been a secret in my family and I just can't have that anymore."

"Why'd you come here?"

"Because she didn't know what happened."

"Who didn't?"

"Your aunt."

"Listen, Mr. Tuttle—"

"Please, call me Jim," he said.

I exhaled. "So look, what is this about exactly?"

"It's about something my father was involved in a long time ago." Tuttle looked out in the direction of the dilapidated house in which the Takahashi family had once lived. "There was another house on the property," he said then. "A little one."

"It's still there," I said. "Not livable but still standing."

"We lived there in 1945," he said then.

"You what now?"

"In the little house," he said. "At least I think it was there. I was only nine years old so I could be wrong."

"The family from Oklahoma," I said simply.

"Yes, that's right. So you know. Maybe you also know that there was a Japanese family, lived in the house before us."

"The Takahashis," I told him.

"That's right. What I need to tell you, or someone, is about the one of them who was a soldier."

"Ray?" I said, practically shouting the name, leaning forward so that poor Jim Tuttle staggered back in alarm. "You mean Ray? Ray Takahashi?"

"Y-y-yes," Tuttle stammered. "That's who I mean. You knew him?"

"I knew his mother well."

And now what passed across his features was unmistakable fear. "Is she still alive?" he said.

"No," I told him, "she passed a couple years ago."

"And Evelyn Wilson is gone as well?"

"That's right."

"And so that leaves you."

"And here I am," I told him.

"Can we go inside? It's awfully hot out here. I wouldn't mind sitting down."

For a moment I was not sure how I should answer, so strange was Jim Tuttle's demeanor, his stammering, sweating lack of surety, as if he had come all this way to tell me some piece of news and yet, now that he had arrived, wanted only to flee. But in the end I held the door open as he staggered into the shaded interior of the house, no cooler inside than out, although at least it was out of the sun and I was able to offer him a cold Coca-Cola, the bottle of which he held to his sweating brow like an ice pack.

We sat at the kitchen table and when he asked me if I was a writer, gesturing to the typewriter with its stack of notes and pages, I evaded the question, telling him I was working on some genealogy, which was not so far from the truth. "I think you'd better tell me what you're doing here," I said to him after it seemed he had settled some, sipping at his Coca-Coca and pulling at his shirt collar.

"I'm not proud of it," he said. "I just want you to know that."

"Okay," I said. "You're not proud of it."

And then I waited as he breathed and drank and set his bottle down and lifted it and drank again and once more returned it to the table. "This is a nice house," he said. "I remember it from when I was a kid. We weren't allowed to come up here but, you know, sometimes my sister and I would sneak around the orchard a little."

"Mr. Tuttle," I said, and then, because he was already gearing up to correct me, "Jim, look, I've got to get back to what I was doing . . ."

"Oh yes, yes," he said. "I'm sorry. I just can't seem to get myself in order." He breathed out slowly and then said, "God give me strength," and then, over the course of the next hour, he told me what I thought I would never know, what I thought no one *could* ever know: what had, in the end, actually happened to Ray Takahashi in 1945 on the night of a rainstorm which would mark the end of that summer and the beginning of the cold gray winter to come.

———

RAY HAD TAKEN TO SLEEPING out on Boulder Ridge with regularity by that time, the heat of August and September drifting into the relative cool of October at last. He lay, most nights, bundled in his greatcoat in the grass, sometimes erecting a small pup tent he carried with him, cooking a can of beans over a fire for his meals and generally living his days increasingly untethered from the world of men. The altercation at the diner had changed things for him, had changed his heart in ways he had not expected or wanted, and yet he did not feel he could leave the place he still, despite everything, felt was his home. When he woke each morning in the boulder-strewn field among the oaks and the squawking blue jays and the small darting shapes of black phoebes and goldfinches and sparrows, he could not help but feel grateful that his eyes had opened here and not upon that other ridge in the French mountains or upon those olive groves in Italy or indeed upon any sky but this one, any trees but these, any grasses but the dry golden grasses of home, a place which he still felt and would ever feel was his birthright.

And yet there would be a reckoning and he knew that too. He had seen them watching him and understood that they watched with purpose and intent. A few days after the incident with Helen in the diner, Ray had come upon a familiar figure on the sidewalk in town. He had already heard, of course, that Chet Kenner had lost his leg in the Pacific but the sight of him there—one pant leg pinned up under his left buttock—was still a shock. Ray was just turning to avoid him when, to his surprise, Chet hailed him as an old friend.

"Listen, Ray," Chet told him after they had finished a round of small talk about the war, their homecoming, the people they knew, "I've been hearing some weird stuff."

"What's that?"

"My brother told me the pickers were talking about you."

"Bish told you that?"

"Yeah, he works out there for the Wilsons, you know."

"I saw him there," Ray said sadly. "What are they saying about me?"

"He wasn't sure," Chet said, "but the fact that they're talking about you at all makes me nervous."

"I'm sure it's nothing," Ray said. "Just pickers blabbing on."

"I hope so." He was silent for a moment and then he said, "Hey maybe you should come stay with us for a few days."

"Stay with you?"

"Well don't make it sound like a thing," Chet said, smiling. "It's not a date."

"Your folks would be okay with that?"

"Shoot, who cares? They'll adjust. One thing about this leg

being gone is my folks will do just about anything I say—at least for now."

Ray stood for a moment in utter silence, staring down the street, the cars moving by with their rattling engines. "That's real nice of you, Chet," he said quietly. "I don't think so, though."

"Where're you sleeping? Outside?"

"Boulder Ridge, mostly," he said.

"Well, shoot, Ray," Chet said then, "the offer stands if you change your mind. Or even if you just want a good meal at a table. Bish would be glad to see you too."

And he could almost see himself there, in some hakujin kitchen in his uniform, with Chet and his younger brother. He had not known Chet well in high school but it was clear now that both he and his younger brother felt that Ray was somehow beyond reproach for the service he had offered to the country, that if no one else cared or acknowledged what Ray had done he at least had these two who looked at him as if he had done something worthwhile. Ray had continued to wear his uniform, as if in living and breathing in that uniform he might yet use it to replace his own flesh so that he would be simply American and nothing else. For was that not why he had first buttoned the shirt over his naked chest, pulled his legs into the trousers, laced his boots? Was that not why he had shot Nazis in France? Was that not why he had watched his companions blown to pieces night after night, day after day, all through southern Europe? Did that not make him, in the end and at long last, American?

"I appreciate that, Chet," he said finally. "But I'm okay out on the ridge."

There had been violence in Placer County, some of it before Ray had returned, and there had been grace as well, hakujin farmers who had kept intact the orchards and farms of their Japanese-American neighbors, returning them, as the Wilsons had promised to do, upon their release from the camps. But there had also been an incident earlier that year where a Japanese-American home had been dynamited and there had been fires that consumed the homes and sheds and equipment of Japanese-Americans all through those golden hills. There would be taunting far into the years to come, Japs and Nips and all the rest. But why these hardscrabble fruit pickers were talking about him—if indeed they were talking about him at all—he could not imagine. Perhaps it was simply more of the same: that Mrs. Wilson had asked them to keep him away from the house. If that was the case, he thought there would be no trouble, since he did not have any reason to go near the house anymore.

He had mentioned to Chet that Jimmy Wilson was dead and Chet told him that it had been in the newspaper and his mother had kept the notice; he would show it to Ray if Ray wanted to see it, although apart from stating that Jimmy had been killed in the Pacific, Chet said that there was nothing in the newsprint that Ray did not already know. The whole world had gone mad for a few years and the boys of that county had thrown themselves into the meat grinder without a thought. Even Ray, for he really had believed that there might be some dispensation for his mother and father and sisters in the camps, that the government might look to his service as a way to release them back to their lives. Nothing he had wanted had come to fruition in the end, the whole of the tree blistering into curl.

———

BY THE TIME THEY CAME he had decided to leave Newcastle entirely, to travel back west toward the Pacific and to find his family in Oakland. Had he left a day earlier, an hour earlier, he might yet have made it, might yet be alive, and then all that could have been might have been, for all of them: his parents, Mrs. Wilson, even Helen. And Franklin, of course; him most of all. Perhaps Ray would have found the boy, would have loved him from afar, watching his son's innocent play from across some Seattle street on a day when the sun shone bright and clear through the clouds. Perhaps the boy would never have known him—for he would have had his own parents, the Yamadas, and assumedly they would have loved him fiercely, having plucked him from that orphanage—but even if they never met, even if Ray never made himself plain and clear to the boy, would not his love have been a kind of shield to him?

The rain was coming on and that grim cold weather had reminded him of that endless night in the Vosges Mountains, sleet descending from a sky so dark that it appeared a depthless slate hovering low above their heads, a darkness punctured by the flat white bursts of the antiaircraft rounds that continued to blast the mountain all around them so that mixed with the sleet were stones and clods of muddy earth. Sometimes blood too would spatter down like some nightmare rain as they huddled together in the cratered foxholes, shivering and chattering and, despite the rain, thirsty beyond measure. For hour after hour he could do little more than lay facedown in the mud, the noise and terror utterly without cease. On either side of him were two men with whom he had crossed much of southern Europe: The others were Victor Fujimori and Jim Ban. Both would die the following day or the day after, although he would not be with them then, and in the dozing half dream of the foxhole they appeared as skeletons in uniform, their death's-head masks grinning out from their helmeted skulls, all around him craters of darkness and of light, the bodies within blooming white and terrible before thudding to earth again, dead, silent, while the big guns continued to fire unabated for all the hours to come. All he could do, despite his training and even despite his will to live, was clutch his helmet, occasionally yelping in fear but otherwise silent, breathless. And the dead. He would remember the dead, especially after the whole of the battle was over and they had accomplished the goal they had set out to accomplish, a goal levied upon them by a general somewhere far afield of where they huddled on that forested mountainside. It was only when the death count came that they would truly understand just how many of them would never leave that French forest. Sometimes Ray wondered if the dead stalked those forests even now, searching out their names in English, in scattered Japanese, their spectral shapes a kind of lambent mist through wet pines.

That he had survived had been a kind of miracle. Now, upon a different ridge, he watched the landscape drift into the quiet of the coming rain, all the beasts of the fields and the birds of the air hunkering down for the weather to come. The fire he built he had already determined would be his last, and so he had used more wood than he ordinarily might, the process of collecting it having brought him to ever-widening circles on that boulder-strewn ridge, the flames now crackling and hissing at the first drops of rain.

When he caught sight of their flashlights dancing up from the road he knew in an instant that the fire had been a mistake. And yet he did not flee but waited there, for in some lit part of his mind he still wondered if it would be Helen come to see him as she had those years before during the course of nights cool and dry and beautiful, her hair in his hands like gold thread in the moonlight and her body warm under his own. It was not until those distant lights flickered off, first one, then the other three, that he felt real fear. He removed the little locket from where he kept it in the front pocket of his uniform trousers and felt its hard, scalloped shape in his hand. He had held it in his palm at Anzio and Cassino and in the Vosges Mountains, held it when the blood and entrails of his companions rained down upon him in the shrapnel hell of those days.

They did not creep in the outer darkness beyond the firelight as he thought they would but came upon him without delay or preamble, their faces drifting before their bodies in the pale, reflected light. He waited, hands at his sides.

Later they would wonder why he had not hunted for a weapon in those moments.

"You know why we come?" one of them said, the sound of his voice dry and lilting with an accent Ray could not identify.

He could see them more clearly now. Three men. They held rifles and he assumed, of course, that the one of their number he could not see, the one who yet crept in the darkness, was similarly armed, and yet he stood with his empty hands by his sides, dirty uniform untucked, frame lit by the fire, watching them impassively as if he had expected them all the while.

"I don't know you," he said simply.

"Damn right you don't," one of the men said. This one was

taller than the others, his neck long and the head above it small and compact, the first of the rain pattering against his hat brim.

"You don't know us fer shit," another said, shorter, barrel-shaped, hatless, thin hair already plastered down from the weight of the water. The third was a nondescript figure, plain and frightened-looking in the shadowy night.

"We're just here on account of we got a job to do," the taller said.

"What job?" Ray said.

"I think you know," the taller said.

For a moment Ray did not speak. Then he said, "Who?"

"I think you know that too," the taller said. "If you don't, you're even dumber than I thought."

"Mrs. Wilson," Ray said.

The man did not respond to this, aside from shifting slightly in his stance. "You shoulda shoved off when you was told," he said.

"Yer too stupid though. Ain't he? He's too stupid." This from the shorter again. The man was practically hopping on his toes with excitement.

Ray was preparing to tell them that he was leaving anyway, that he would pack up and leave that moment if only to avoid a fight of such numbers and such odds, but this last had set his teeth hard together in his mouth. He squared his shoulders against the whole of it. "Shut your goddamn mouth," he said.

"We heard you had a temper on you," he said.

"Just leave me alone," Ray said. "Just leave me the hell alone."

"Too late for that," the shorter said. "What you gonna do, Jap?" The short one swung the rifle around so that it pointed at him.

He almost laughed then at the absurdity of his situation, that he would come through all of it—the unsettlement of the camps, the fire and terror of the war—and was now here, in the orange light of a campfire upon a ridge which he had come to think of as his and Helen's, their place together upon which he had ranged over the secret geography of her body.

"I don't like you pointing that at me," Ray said quietly, his voice steady, although there was a trembling inside of him. That it would come to this. That it ever could have.

"I don't give a rat shit," the short one said, then added, as if a nursery rhyme: "Jap shit, rat shit."

"Christ, Tuck," the tall man said, his head shaking quickly in disgust. "Let's just get this done."

There was no more talking. The two men held their rifles on him as the tall man tied his hands behind his back with a length of coarse rope. When the knot was finished the tall man gave a whistle and the fourth man appeared from the darkness. It was he who gave the first blow, leaning in and calling him a dirty Jap and then striking again. For a time Ray tried to remain standing but it was too much and when he fell to the grass it was as if he were a pillar of ash come crumbling into the rain. That it was cool against his face was a blessing, for the blows continued and they were too many to count: his face exploding in agony, his thighs, his back, his neck, his chest, even his bound wrists. Their fists; then their boots.

"Point is, Jap," someone whispered in his ear, "you'd best clear out or we'll finish the job."

"We ought just finish," another said.

"I ain't a murderer," the first voice said. "Anyway, that's not what we got paid for."

"She's just a girl," the other said. "She don't know what she wants."

He felt himself rise through the delirium of his pain at this, like a thick jelly pushing up toward the airborne light just above the surface of the sea. "A girl?" he said. His face felt numb, and there was a warm wetness in his mouth. A hard jagged stone there which he knew must be a broken shard of tooth.

"What'd he say?" someone mumbled. And then, louder: "What'd you say, Jap?"

His voice was a struggle. "A girl? What girl?"

"Shit, Tuck," a voice said. "He don't even know. How's that for it? He don't even know who he's got to thank. Boy, you really are up shit creek without a paddle."

"God," Ray said now, his heart lurching so hard and heavy that it felt for a moment as if it might break clear from his ribs, not like an arrow but like an egg, its viscous ooze soaking through him and into the grass.

"The old lady paid us," a voice said calmly, "but it's the daughter who wants it done."

"You sons of bitches," Ray said then. "You goddamn sons of bitches." He tried to rise then, struggling against them as they came, the rope somehow loose so that his hands were before him and he was swinging in a wide arc and somehow connecting, first one fell and then another and he had to get away, from the men, from the ridge, from the Wilsons, from the whole of the map of his life, and so he spun from the campfire and ran, a staggering, loping figure, maniacal for motion itself and possessed only of that singular thought: to get away, to get away, to get away.

When the shot rang out he did not know what it was,

although he had heard so much gunfire in his life, more than anyone had any right to, but not here. His body jerked forward as if it had been shoved from behind, as if some benevolent hand were helping propel him. From somewhere a shouted voice: "No, goddammit!" and already he was falling, for his legs were empty of whatever had moved them, whatever had pushed them on.

In the palm of his hand he could feel it, for he had held it all the while, even during the worst of it, even when the men had tied his hands and beaten him. He had gone down to his knees in the grass and now the grass seemed to pull him into its embrace and he let himself into it, his thumb on the locket, tracing its scalloped shape. When he looked back it was to see four faces outlined against a sky awash with black clouds. He wondered who they might be and thought they might offer some sense of where he was headed but when they spoke he could make no sense of it at all.

—Goddammit, Tuck, you done kilt him.

—He was runnin'.

—Of course he was runnin', you idiot. We was beatin' on him. You'da run too.

—Shoot. Only a Jap anyway.

—Now we gotta dig. And it's rainin' cats and dogs.

—I'll get the shovels.

—He was runnin'. What else I s'posed to do? He was runnin' away.

—That was the whole goddamn point. He was s'posed to run away. That's what she paid us for.

And so the last words he ever heard. Above him, the slate of clouded sky continued to recede and the men leaned over what had become a kind of black tunnel cut into the air, their faces and the clouds all at the far end of it, the whole of that sky fleeing from him so that the thought that came at the very end was that he was lost, but when he turned his head he saw that he was, all the while, winging out toward some other sky, a vast plane of deepest blue which was yet familiar to him, more familiar than the world he had just departed, and he knew it was a kind of homecoming and that homecoming was bright and golden and its hills rolled on forever and his heart burst at the sight of that pure blessed land.

———

THE BONES OF THIS ARE what Jim Tuttle told me that afternoon, although of course I have imagined aspects of his story that no one will ever know. Tuttle's father had been the one stalking the darkness, just outside the range of faint orange light from the campfire. "That man Tucker was a bad man," Tuttle told me. "Ended up in Folsom Prison for murder later on."

"No one turned him in?" I asked him.

"Wasn't their way," he said sadly. "Look, Mr. Frazier, I'm a Christian. Born again, you might say, and I just don't want that blemish on my conscience."

"Your dad told you all this?"

"When he was dying," Tuttle said, nodding. "Told me he was afraid he'd go to hell."

"Did he pull the trigger?"

"That man Tucker did."

"And they buried him out there?"

"That's what he said. I don't know where exactly. Would help complete things to have him moved into a Christian cemetery but there's no way to find him now. I tried. It's just grass and boulders and trees and not much else. All looks the same."

"He was Buddhist," I said, as if this somehow addressed his concern.

"Still, seems wrong for him to be out there alone," Tuttle said in response.

When he was leaving, Jim Tuttle stopped in my doorway and reached into his shirt pocket, the movement of his thick fingers awkward and raking, but he came out with what he intended to find there, a length of silver chain upon which something dangled, a kind of pendant. "I don't know if this'd mean anything to you," he said.

"What is it?"

"My dad said the soldier had it in his hand."

I thanked Jim Tuttle for coming. He handed me a card with an address and his phone number and then I stood there on the porch, watching him drive away. From somewhere upstairs came the knocking of a hammer on a nail, a scatter of voices from outside. All that which had disappeared during the telling of Tuttle's story now drifted back into the living world once more.

I did not uncurl my fist until I had reached the dining room table again, taking my seat at the typewriter and only then gazing with attention at what Jim Tuttle had given me. The chain was delicate but not particularly so and the locket a small shell-shaped piece of metal, silver in color but likely tin, with small dents and scratches here and there from the years. It was difficult to open but I managed, at last, to pry the lid free and sat staring down at the tiny image that might well have been Evelyn

Wilson once upon a time but which was, of course, Helen. The woman encased in the shell-shaped tin was faint, the image granular, but where her mother contained within her a fierce beauty this girl was plain, ordinary, and yet she had filled Ray Takahashi's heart so fully that he held her image with him for all the days of his imprisonment at the camps and all the days of war and held it still upon his return to what he thought, up to the last, was his home. That it had been Helen, and not her mother, who had at last hired the men to chase Ray out of her life was as terrible as it was believable, for was she not, in the end, her mother's daughter?

———

THE HOUSE IS FINISHED NOW, or as finished as it will ever be, since I have more or less run out of the necessary funds for continuing its renovation. Perhaps this is a blessing, since I have come to understand that there is no end to such tasks, the process of replacing and rebuilding such that one wonders if the object that remains is still itself; if you replace every board of a house is it still the same house or something else? The work I had done here is not quite so drastic as that but it has been enough to make me feel, in some way, as if the house is now mine, even though the furniture remains more or less where it was when I first entered the parlor. Now my daughter charges through its rooms and up and down its stairs and lets its screen door clack shut with a terrific bang. The three of us have occupied the house in the way a family occupies a house, making a series of rooms and stairs and hallways into a home by the act of simply being in them, of stirring whatever ghosts remain, most of them fleeing out through the new shingles and into the blue summer night.

I informed a sheriff's deputy of what I knew of Raymond Takahashi's murder, although I well know it will likely come to nothing—a thirty-eight-year-old case without a body and without a living perpetrator is of little interest to the law—and yet I felt duty-bound to do that much. I also wrote Doris Harris, née Takahashi, whose address I still have, to tell her the story. Into that envelope I slipped the pendant. It was never mine, although in some ways I know it is not Doris's either. The actions of sealing that envelope and dropping it at the post office have been two of the most difficult of my life, although I lack the words to explain why, even to myself.

Sometimes I can still feel the Wilsons in the rooms and halls and the stairwell of this old house, not only Evelyn and Homer but the children too, Jimmy and Helen in the upstairs bedrooms, bright phantoms whose yellow days extend into our own. How they shimmer like tinsel in the air. And Ray of course, in the days in which he was yet a child and could not even imagine all the madness that would descend in the years to come. Their laughter like bells. Their breath sweet with fruit.

And of course there are other shadows here as well and a good many of them are my own. This place has been handed to me utterly without warrant: the house, the old orchard trees, even the remains of the home in which the Takahashi family once lived. It is difficult not to feel that the whole of it represents the spoils of some war in which I was, wittingly and unwittingly, a participant. Ray Takahashi's bones are lost in the earth somewhere on Boulder Ridge even now, even as you read these words, his family inexorably changed in the aftermath of that incontrovertible fact. That the family was not destroyed by what the Wilsons—by what my family—did to them, a series of actions built upon a legacy of sanctioned violence both subtle and overt, is but a testament to their strength. And perhaps it is, too, a comment on my own weakness that, despite everything, I choose to live here with my own family, to occupy this place, a place which I have, in no conceivable way, earned.

Sometimes, when I fail to find my dreams, I sit at the upstairs window in what I still think must have been Helen's room, a room which we have used only for storage. I have placed a chair under the window and it is here that I sit some nights, my daughter asleep in her own room and my dear wife asleep in our bed. I have said that I do this when I fail to find my dreams but in reality it is my dreams I am avoiding, for there remains, in the darker of my nights, a patch of rough water that runs through my thoughts, one which I recognize well enough to know that were I to drift into sleep under its influence I would find myself in the seeping heat again even after all these years. I light a cigarette and look out at the cool quietude of the night. On the opposite ridge, the roof of the little house in which the Takahashis once lived is like a slightly crooked line set upon the softness of the night canopy of the trees. What I think of there, what I am horrified to admit to, is that my location is a perfect one from which to call in an air strike. One-zero-Sierra. Foxtrot-Juliett. Six-zero. Two-seven. Zero-five. Three-six. And all of this would be transmuted into flame. It is, I think, a calling for relief more than anything else, for each time the heavy concussion came I could feel my heart unspooling in gratitude and deliverance.

My wife sometimes finds me in my chair, asleep, my cigarette an ash column between my fingers. She rouses me and sometimes we return to bed; other times, if my daughter is awake, we all head downstairs and pour our bowls of cereal and begin our day. Suzie is six years old and she is filled with questions and I try to answer them as I crunch my Chex and sip my coffee. Later the three of us will walk through the oaks and the last peaches and plums and despite everything I have done and all the guilt I carry both inherited and earned, despite it or perhaps because of it, I know that I am lucky, not only to be alive, but to have found in my life a measure of grace, or rather for that measure to have found me. There are days—many of them— when golden light seems to pour forth from the very soil. That I am here to meet that light continues to amaze. Somewhere phantoms yet blaze the sky. And yet what I think of most is this:

Sweet life. Have you not been with me all the while?

ACKNOWLEDGMENTS

I GREW UP IN PLACER COUNTY AND LIVE, NOW, IN THE TOWN I have fictionalized herein. It has been a singular honor, therefore, to be trusted with the recollections of the various Placer County citizens who gave me their time, attention, memories, photographs, and reference materials. Thanks to Ray and Irene Yamasaki (and Denise Yamasaki for helping me connect with her parents); to Shig Yokote of the 442nd, whom I was fortunate enough to speak with just a few months shy his one hundredth birthday about his experiences before, during, and after the war (and double fortunate to join him later for the birthday party); to Stu Kageta, who shared his own experiences and those of his father, Frank, a machine gunner in the 442nd; and to Claire Camp (née Tsujimoto) for inviting me into her home and for her input and comments and her loan of some essential books on Tule Lake. Ken Tokutomi provided early guidance and contacts and made a rough sketch of the old Newcastle Japantown so I could begin to get my bearings around that vanished topography. Further to that study, Bill George's documentary film *Newcastle, Gem of the Foothills* provided context and narratives of a lost time.

Dan Wilson kindly gathered some old Placer High School yearbooks for me so that I might be availed of the photographic evidence of Placer County's demographics before and after the war. Local historian David Unruhe, a contributing editor to *The Japantowns of Placer County*, offered his time, suggestions, knowledge, and contacts—and a big stack of books and files from his personal collection—and Mike Holmes kindly offered me his research file on local events just after internment. Also useful were the collections of the Auburn branch of the Placer County Library—especially their oral history collection—and the holdings of the Placer County Archives. Paul DeWitt kindly assisted me on a tour of the Japanese American Museum of San Jose, patiently answering my many questions.

Among the dozens of textual sources consulted during the research for this book, the most useful were Wayne Maeda's *Changing Dreams and Treasured Memories: A Story of Japanese Americans in the Sacramento Region* and Sierra College Press's outstanding collection of Placer County oral histories, *Standing Guard: Telling Our Stories*. Tomeo Okui Nakae's *Recollections: An Autobiography of the Wife of a Japanese Immigrant* provided useful information on life in Newcastle during the first half of the twentieth century. The writings of Mary Matsuda Gruenewald, Hiroshi Kashiwagi, Donald Keene, Julie Otsuka, Eileen Sunada Sarasohn, Hisaye Yamamoto, and Wakako Yamauchi were also important. The list of family names to whom this book is dedicated was extracted from the *Tule Lake Directory and*

Camp News compiled and published by H. Inukai and supplied to me by the rangers at the Tule Lake Unit of WWII Valor in the Pacific National Monument, in Tulelake, California.

My friend William T. Vollmann kindly accompanied me to the UC Davis library several times and helped me research agricultural events in California from 1920 until the peach and pear blight wiped out much of the state's fruit-growing industry in the early 1960s.

I would also like to offer my appreciation to members of two literary conference panels which focused on writers crossing outside their lived experiences and which gave me much to think about as I pondered how to approach this story: Jodi Angel, Skip Horack, Bich Minh Nguyen, Derek Palacio, Rob Spillman, Luis Alberto Urrea, and Naomi Williams. I would also like to thank Matthew Salesses, whose engaging pedagogical work, particularly on the subject of white writers writing about people of color, has been eye-opening and useful, as has the work of Viet Thanh Nguyen, especially *Nothing Ever Dies: Vietnam and the Memory of War*, which offered ways to consider America's treatment and understanding of Asia both inside and outside its borders. Edward W. Said's *Orientalism* and *Culture and Imperialism* and Judith Butler's *Frames of War: When Is Life Grievable?* were important to me as I framed how to handle these same subjects.

On the American experience in Vietnam, I found useful sources in Joseph W. Callaway Jr.'s *Mekong First Light*, Andrew Wiest's *The Boys of '67*, Frederick Downs Jr.'s *The Killing Zone*, Michael Herr's *Dispatches*, and Nick Turse's *Kill Anything That Moves: The Real American War in Vietnam*. Also important was Liz Reph's documentary *Brothers in War*. Special thanks too for the memoir *In Pharaoh's Army* and to its author, Tobias Wolff, for his kindness in looking over my pages on the Vietnam War and spending some time in discussion with me over email. In terms of naming the nameless, a task my protagonist was never able to do, the reader might explore Dương Thu Hương's *Paradise of the Blind* and *Novel Without a Name*, Hữu Ngọc's *Wandering Through Vietnamese Culture*, Bảo Ninh's *The Sorrow of War*, Nguyễn Huy Thiệp's *The General Retires and Other Stories*, Nguyễn Ngọc Tư's *Floating Lives*, Heonik Kwon's *Ghosts of War in Vietnam*, and the anthologies *Wild Mustard: New Voices from Vietnam* (edited by Charles Waugh, Nguyễn Lien, and Văn Giá), *Night, Again* (edited by Linh Dinh), and *Vietnam: A Traveler's Literary Companion* (edited by John Balaban and Nguyen Qui Duc).

I would particularly like to thank Marie Mutsuki Mockett and Naomi Williams for their attention to questions of Japanese culture, character, and language. For support and care: Tetuzi Akiyama, Marcelo Hernandez Castillo, Alexander Chee, and Emily Nemens. Special thanks to Michael Spurgeon and Jonathan Franzen for helping me find those moments when the unruly eccentricities of my sentences tilted toward the unreadable.

To my agent and dear friend Eleanor Jackson: much love and gratitude for everything you have done and for all you continue to do and, in particular, for continuing to have faith in my work, even when I can't find such faith for myself. My editor at Liveright is Katie Adams, a true genius who could somehow see what I was trying to do here in the midst of what I first gave her to read: an unwieldly and impossibly entangled narrative. Katie, you make my work better every time but this book you absolutely rescued. To the rest of team Liveright, especially Cordelia Calvert and Gina Iaquinta: my sincere gratitude.

Of the 110,000 people of Japanese ancestry displaced under Executive Order 9066, 18,789 were imprisoned behind barbed wire at the 7,400-acre concentration camp at Tule Lake. Today, the site of the camp is little more than a desolate field of dry grass through which the wreckage of concrete foundations can barely be seen. The field is once more surrounded by barbed wire and the weekday I visited, with my friend the writer Debra Gwartney, there was no ranger available to open its locked gate. Somehow this seemed fitting enough: the impossibility of entering that space, its fence meant to keep us out, rather than to keep anyone locked inside.

This book is for the families and descendants of those who survived. It is also for my wife Macie and for my children. If there is any grace in my life it is because of you.